Gordon DeMarco was raised in Akron, Ohio. He went to San Francisco in 1967 to attend graduate school at San Francisco State College. There, he became a participant in the 1968–69 student strike and co-chairperson of Students for a Democratic Society (SDS). Since that time he has worked as a dishwasher, a chauffeur, a docker, a worker in a puppet centre and a supply teacher.

His other books include *Polish September* (on Solidarity), *The Canvas Prison*, and *October Heat*, which introduced Riley Kovachs. He has recently completed a play entitled *Who's Afraid of Abbie Hoffman*.

Pluto Crime

Edited by Ronald Segal

Murder in the Central Committee	Manuel Vázquez Montalban
October Heat	Gordon DeMarco
The China Option	Nancy Milton
Morbid Symptoms	Gillian Slovo
The Waste Remains	Judith Cook
Junk on the Hill	Jeremy Pikser
Dance Hall of the Dead	Tony Hillerman
Days Like These	Nigel Fountain
Watching the Detectives	Julian Rathbone
The Dark Red Star	Ivan Ruff
Operation Emerald	Dominic McCartan

'. . . Is there anything inherently illogical with the concept of socialist – or, at least, politically and socially aware – crime fiction? Pluto Press, publishers of serious left wing books, have inaugurated a crime list to prove that the two can mix . . . the first batch of pinko whodunits augurs well for the genre.' *The Times*

'. . . the most innovative publishing experiment of the crime-story year!' *The Guardian*

Gordon DeMarco

Frisco Blues

Pluto Press
London and Sydney

First published in 1985 by Pluto Press Limited,
The Works, 105a Torriano Avenue, London NW5 2RX
and Pluto Press Australia Limited, PO Box 199, Leichhardt,
New South Wales 2040, Australia

7 6 5 4 3 2 1
89 88 87 86 85

Phototypeset by AKM Associates (UK) Ltd,
Ajmal House, Hayes Road, Southall, London
Printed in Great Britain by Cox & Wyman,
Cardiff Road, Reading, Berks

British Library Cataloguing in Publication Data
DeMarco, Gordon
Frisco blues. —— (Pluto crime)
I. Title
813'.54[F] PR6054.4/

ISBN 0 7453 0042 1
ISBN 0 7453 0040 5 Pbk

1.

I was sitting at the counter at the Chat 'n Chew, a one-armed joint on Mission at 25th. I had just polished off a plate of eggs and hash-browns. Lucy, the waitress, was pouring me a refill when I heard a voice from over my shoulder.

'Mr Kovachs?'

'Yeah, I said, turning my head. She was young, maybe 22 or 23 at most. Her skin was the color of roasted chestnut shells and she was dressed entirely in black.

'Mr Kovachs,' she said, in a tiny voice that trembled slightly, 'I would like to talk to you. Please.'

I got up from the stool, took my cup in hand and motioned her to a back booth. 'We can talk over there,' I said. 'Would you like some coffee?' She shook her head: no. We sat in the booth facing each other. There followed a brief, uneasy silence. 'What can I do for you, Miss?'

'I'm no Miss,' she said, looking down at the handbag she held in her lap. 'And now I'm not a Mrs, either,' she added, her voice trailing off to almost nothing.

'I'm afraid I don't understand.

She continued staring at her handbag. 'My name is Ruby Jones. My husband was Chet Jones.'

'Was?'

'He's dead now, Mr Kovachs.' Ruby Jones reached in and pulled out a small white handkerchief from her pocketbook and held it up to her eyes. She sobbed quietly.

'I'm sorry, Mrs Jones.'

For a moment Ruby Jones just sat there with her eyes covered. It was all very awkward. Then she blew her nose and regained her composure as if the last few minutes had never happened.

'I apologize, Mr Kovachs. You see, I've just come from the cemetery.'

I held up my hands. 'No need to explain, Mrs Jones.'

'They said it was his fault, Mr Kovachs. They said Chet was careless, that's why he fell.'

'I'm sorry, Mrs Jones, but I'm not following you. What is it you're trying to tell me?'

Lucy came over and poured me another cup without asking. I shook out a Chesterfield from my shirt pocket and lit it up.

'Chet was working at Pacific Shipyard, Mr Kovachs. He was painting a hull from a scaffold. The scaffold broke and he fell 70 feet to the pier. The doctors said it was a broken neck. The company said it was Chet's fault. They said he was new on the job and didn't know how to handle the ropes of the scaffolding.'

'You didn't buy that did you, Mrs Jones?'

'Chet knew just about all there was to know about ships, Mr Kovachs. It's true that he was new on the job, but he knew how to handle scaffolding. It was old and broke. It's the company's fault.'

I took a gulp of Lucy's coffee and swirled it around my mouth for a moment before swallowing it. 'Why are you telling me all this, Mrs Jones?'

'I need someone to help me, Mr Kovachs. I've got two kids to feed. Chet and I were very happy together, but we weren't very well off, if you know what I mean.'

'You should see a lawyer if you want to file a suit against the shipyard.'

'I thought of that, Mr Kovachs. But what I need is someone who can, you know, get something on this company, before I can think of taking them to court. I talked to the union lawyer – Chet was a warehouseman – and he told me they had been trying to get something on the company for years, but have never been able to. He told me it would take years and then I'd probably lose.'

'Not much in the way of encouragement, is it?'

'Mr Kovachs, Chet was killed because that company was too damn cheap to keep its equipment in shape. Chet told me that himself nearly every day. "Someday, Ruby," he would tell me, "somebody's going to get killed there."' Her voice trailed off again.

'I really don't see what I can do, Mrs Jones.'

'Mr Kovachs, I've got two kids and no job and no family to help me. I think this company owes me something. Damn it, they didn't even say they were sorry.' An alarm sparked off in Ruby Jones's eyes. There was a fire burning out of control.

'Why did you come to *me*, Mrs Jones?'

'You're known around the ILWU as somebody to trust. I'd rather have a colored man working for me, and for Chet's sake, but I'm no fool. A Negro snooping around a shipyard trying to find something dirty on the company. How far do you think he would get? He'd be one dead nigger, Mr Kovachs. And that's all Chet is to them.'

'I guess I could nose around a bit. I know a welder who works for Pacific. Maybe he knows something. I'm not promising anything, you understand. But I'll ask a few questions.'

A smile came to Ruby Jones's face. 'Thank you, Mr Kovachs. I was told I could count on you.'

'I got a fan club or what? Who told you I was old trusty?'

'Oh, just some of the boys around the union hall. Your name came up. I didn't ask questions. I'm desperate. I'd be talking to Edgar Bergen and Charley McCarthy if their names came up, but they didn't.'

'Well, with that extraordinary vote of confidence, how can I refuse?'

Ruby Jones opened her purse and began fishing around in it. 'How much do you charge, Mr Kovachs?'

I reached across the table and took her hand out of her pocket book. 'Look, I said I'd ask a few questions. That's all. No charge for asking a couple of questions.'

Ruby Jones screwed up her face. 'I'm not a charity case, Mr Kovachs. Chet and me always paid our own way.'

'Yes, but there's no Chet now. Look, if I turn up something and it gets you some insurance money from Pacific, we'll talk about it then. How about that?'

Ruby Jones smiled with her eyes. 'Well, that might do. But only if we put it in writing. Like I said, I'm no charity case and I don't want nobody working for me just because he's sorry for me.'

I didn't want to argue with pride and allowed her to write out the terms of an agreement between us. She had me sign and date it. She folded it up and put it in her purse. I asked her for the names of some of her husband's friends and co-workers. I told her that I would check back with her the next morning. She got up and left the Chat 'n Chew. I watched her cross the street and board a Mission Street bus. I continued to stare out the window for another few minutes. 'What have I gotten myself into?' I asked the napkin holder on the table.

2.

I finished off the last two gulps of Lucy's murk before going to work. I drove down to the Pacific Shipyards at Pier 50. It was 11.30 a.m. by my watch. I took a little walk down to the Third Street drawbridge and back while waiting for the noon whistle to blow. If I knew Bill Whitney, a friend from the old days and a welder at Pacific, he would be among the first through the gate. The whistle blew at high noon and less than two minutes later Whitney was walking through the gate.

'Bill!' I shouted across the 30 feet of pavement and gravel separating us. He turned his head without breaking his brisk stride. He was looking in my direction but hadn't recognized me. I held up my hand and called his name again. By that time I was only ten paces away and directly in front of him.

'Riley!' he said, truly astonished. 'What are you doing down here? Come to take my place for the afternoon, I hope?'

'Sorry, old man. Nothing like that, I'm afraid.'

'Aw, come on,' he said poking me in the ribs. 'I'll even let you use my hood.'

'Well, it is tempting,' I said feigning seriousness.

'This welding is for the birds. The birds! I can't decide whether to croak from all the junk I've inhaled into my lungs or just settle for a case of hemorrhoids.'

Bill Whitney had been a welder for the past six or seven years. And for the last three he had been trying to get out. He claimed welding had given him the body of a man 15 years older than his 35 years. Sometimes, he looked it.

'This is business, Bill,' I said. 'No time to sit and reminisce about the welding profession. Mission Rock?' I pointed in the direction of the pierside restaurant and bait store five minutes down the road.

'Lead the way,' he said. 'The farther away we get from this place, the better I like it.'

Over a couple of Polish hot dogs, both eaten by Bill, and some beer, I told him of my conversation with Mrs Ruby Jones. He listened intently while wolfing down the Polish, occasionally squirting juice when he bit into the sausage skin. I asked if he knew anything about Chet Jones's death.

'It's a big tub, Riley,' he said, referring to the *Hawaii Princess*, the ship he was working on. He wiped the mustard from the corners of his mouth with a paper napkin and took a hearty swallow of beer. 'There's got to be 300 guys working on her. Sure, I heard about the guy falling off the scaffold.'

'Company told Mrs Jones her husband was a new man and didn't know how to handle the equipment.'

'Sure. What do you expect them to say? Jones was the third man killed at Pacific this year. The other two had 23 years' experience between them. The company said they didn't know how to handle the equipment either.'

'Same old story, eh?'

'Yeah. The working conditions there are gruesome. Always have been. The company always claims accidents are caused by "human error". Shit, Riley, the human error is in the goddamn executive suite. You and me and 300 other guys know that.'

'Doesn't sound too good for Mrs Jones, does it? She's trying to get the company to pay out for her husband's death.'

'I heard the union filed a claim. But they filed claims for the widows of Blaine and McIntire – the two guys who were killed earlier – and so far they haven't seen dollar one. Oh, she might win in the courts, but it could take years.'

'That's what the union lawyer told her. Blaine and McIntire – were they white?'

'Yeah. What are you driving at?'

'Jones was a Negro. I thought there might be a discrimination thing involved.'

'It's hard to tell, Riley. Lousy working conditions cut across race lines at Pacific.' Bill Whitney knocked back the last of his beer. 'But I'll tell you one thing. Something's been going on in the yard the past month or so. Something ugly.'

'Yeah? What?'

'Prejudice is on the rise. You know the history of the Boilermakers. They had Jim Crow locals until two years ago. Well, there's been a couple of incidents. Mainly just the old harassment stuff. You know, white guys calling the colored guys "niggers". Stuff like that. But it's been happening a lot lately. And it's mainly coming from the same bunch of rowdies. Gladiator types. You know, hard-noses who're always looking for a reason to pick a fight.'

'Do you know if Chet Jones was involved in any of these incidents?'

'Can't say for sure. But there was a big rumble at lunch last week. Nearly every Negro worker in the yard was involved. Just a lot of shoving, but it could have gotten real ugly if you know what I mean.' Bill Whitney got up from his chair. 'Look, Riley, I've got to get back to work. Got to inhale some more of that wonderful stuff if I am going to screw up my lungs properly.'

'One last thing, Bill. There might not be anything there, but I'd like to talk with some of the Negro workers. Preferably friends of the dead man. Think you can arrange it?'

'Don't know. Like I said, things have been pretty tense

lately. I do know this guy, Williams. We used to eat lunch together sometimes before all this started. But now, I don't know if he will talk to me, let alone, you.'

'Could you give it a try?'

'Sure, I'll try. Look, Riley, I've really got to go. Unless you want to take me up on my offer. The hood.' He dangled his welder's hood in front of me and smiled.

'I'll call you around six.'

'Spoil sport.' Bill Whitney put on his metal safety hat, lit up a smoke, gave me a very sloppy salute and walked out of the cafe.

I finished my beer then walked over to the public fishing pier next to Mission Rock. A couple of kids straight out of *Huckleberry Finn* were sitting on the edge, their socks and shoes off and pants rolled up to the knees, with long poles between their legs. Their lines dangled lazily in the muddy bay waters. They didn't seem to be in any hurry to catch a fish. Just passing the time of their youth.

I looked across the water to Oakland and Berkeley. A rock quarry in East Oakland and the Campanile at the University were the only shapes I could identify through the light brown foggy haze. A quarter of a mile down the pier on the Frisco side of the Bay, I took a look at the *Hawaii Princess* berthed in the Pacific yard like a beached whale. 'Three deaths in less than a year,' I said through my teeth. So much for the romance of the sea.

3.

I spent the early part of the afternoon talking with one of the lawyers for the longshoremen's union. Concerning Mrs Jones's chances to collect death benefits from Pacific, he told me nothing I didn't already know. He said the union was calling for an investigation into the deaths of the three men killed at Pacific, but since the ILWU had only a few men working in the yard, he wasn't too optimistic.

He told me his union and some of the marine metal trade locals were making safety a number-one issue in the next contract. He said he was convinced conditions would improve, not just at Pacific, but all up and down the coast. That was well and good, but it wouldn't help Mrs Jones and her two fatherless kids. And that was my concern.

There was nothing I could do until evening so I spent the rest of the afternoon at the movies. I saw *Crossfire*. It was a story about prejudice and anti-semitism. It starred Robert Ryan. It wasn't a great movie, as movies go, but it was pretty bold stuff coming from Hollywood, considering its yearly tonnage of cowboy shoot-'em-ups and Fred Astaire musicals.

I returned to my dump a little past 6 p.m. and called Bill Whitney. He told me he spoke with Williams, but it didn't go too well. He said the Negro workers were in a pretty angry mood and were reluctant to have anything to do with whites.

'It's a pretty touchy situation down there, right now,' he said. 'The ILWU is trying to calm things down. There's a joint shop stewards meeting tomorrow to deal with it.

But as good a record as the longshoremen have on the race issue, they're a pretty small unit inside the yard, and besides, it only takes a few hotheads to set things off.'

'What about Williams?' I asked. 'Will he talk to me?'

'He told me he didn't want to talk to anybody. But he did give me his phone number. So maybe there's a chance. He's a good man, Riley, but he's hurt. All the Negro workers down there are hurting over this thing. They're angry, too.'

Whitney gave me Williams's phone number. I told him to stay in touch. I turned on the radio and listened to the rest of Gabriel Heater and the first few minutes of the *Darts for Dough* quiz program before calling Williams.

A throaty baritone voice at the other end said 'Yeah' before the phone had rung three times.

'Mr Williams?' I said.

'Yeah. Who is you?'

'My name's Kovachs. I believe Bill Whitney spoke to you about me.'

'Uh huhnh.'

'Did he tell you that I'm working for Chet Jones's widow?'

'Uh huhnh.'

'You probably know that the company has refused to pay her any death benefits.'

'Uh huhnh.'

'She thought I might be able to turn up something that would prove the company was responsible for her husband's accident.'

'Uh huhnh.'

'Mr Williams, do you have any information about Chet Jones's death? Or names of witnesses to the accident?'

'Wasn't no accident.' The phone went dead.

I dialed again. Williams answered. 'We got cut off, Mr Williams,' I said.

'I hung up.'

'Look, Mr Williams. I know this must be rough for you, but I want to help Mrs Jones, if I can.'

'You can help by sticking your nose out from where it don't belong.' The phone went dead again. I dialed Williams's number for the third time. I let it ring 15 times before coming to the obvious conclusion that Mr Williams was no longer home. At least not to me.

I was going to forget the whole thing and settle in for a night at the radio with Jimmy Durante, The Great Guildersleeve, and maybe Mr District Attorney, but something Williams had said stuck to the back of my throat like peanut butter. 'Wasn't no accident.' Those were his exact words. I thought he had meant no accident as in the company was knowingly at fault by having old, unsafe equipment for the men to work with. It was probably exactly what he meant, but I could only be sure if I could pry a few more sentences out of him. And that seemed unlikely.

I turned down the radio, missing the last verse of *Ink-a-Dink-Do* and dialed Mrs Jones. I told her I hadn't been able to turn up a thing that would give her any encouragement. Then I told her about my conversation, such as it was, with Williams and said there was the thinnest thread he might know something if I could get him to talk. She said she knew him and would get him to speak with me. She was a very confident lady.

I really didn't expect to hear from her until the next afternoon, but Ruby Jones phoned me less than an hour later and told me to come to her house in 20 minutes. Williams would be there.

Twenty minutes later I was knocking at the door of her Fillmore district flat. She let me in without saying a word and escorted me down a narrow hallway to a small living room. There, sitting on the sofa was a large, muscular Negro man about 45 years old. He was the color of a cup of coffee with nothing added and his face was as ridged and leathery as the trunk of a tree.

'Mr Kovachs,' Mrs Jones said, standing between me and the seated man, 'this is Levi Williams.'

I stuck out my hand, but Williams just sat stiffly on the couch. 'I'm only here 'cause of Ruby and the kids,' he said sullenly.

'Now, Levi!' said Mrs Jones. 'You promised you would help me.'

'I'm here, ain't I?' he said.

'Well, you can begin by losing that bad attitude of yours. Mr Kovachs is here to help me, too.'

I held up my hand to interrupt Ruby Jones. 'Mr Williams. Earlier, on the phone, you said Mr Jones's death wasn't an accident. What did you mean?'

Levi Williams looked at Ruby Jones, then at me and finally at the floor.

'Go on, Levi,' Ruby Jones insisted. 'Tell the man what you told me.'

He looked hard into her eyes for a moment before turning to me. 'I mean Chet didn't die of no accident. That's what I mean. He was killed.'

'Killed?' I said. 'You mean murdered?'

'Same thing, ain't they?'

'How? Who?'

Levi Williams looked at Mrs Jones.

'Go on, Levi,' she said. 'Tell him. Tell him everything you told me.'

'Don't boss me, woman,' Levi Williams said raising his voice. He took his time reaching inside his coat for a cigarette. 'Get me a light, Ruby.'

She dug into the pocket of her dress, took out a book of matches and handed them across the sofa to him. He tore one off and struck it. When the cigarette was going, he was ready to talk.

'First off, mister,' he said, 'I don't know who you is. Bill Whitney says you're okay and Ruby here says you're okay. Well, I don't know nothin' 'bout you. I'm keepin' my eye on you. Till I know better, you ain't nothin' but trouble.'

'Levi, please!' Ruby Jones exclaimed impatiently.

'I said I'd tell him. Now be still.'

Levi Williams took a long drag from his cigarette. 'Whitney told you 'bout the goin's on down at Pacific?' I nodded. 'Then you know they is some bad blood between the whites and the coloreds.' Again I nodded. 'Well, they is two dozen crackers that's mostly been causin' all this mess. They been makin' life miserable for us ever since they come home from the war. Most white boys on the docks treats us fair and don't mind workin' next to a black man, but some of 'em just as soon slit our throats open as be caught in the same part of town. You know what I'm talkin' 'bout?'

I nodded. Levi Williams took his pack of cigarettes from his shirt pocket, took one and laid the pack on the small coffee table separating us. He pushed the pack toward me. 'Here, take one,' he said coolly. 'You look like you could use one.' He paused. 'Things wasn't never real good in the shipyards. Especially in the Boilermakers. Even during the war they tried all kinds of things to keep us down. But things has been a whole lot better since that mess over at Marinship ended and the court told them to integrate their lodges. Things was just about tolerable. That is, until about two months ago.'

'What happened then?' I interrupted.

'I'm fixin' to tell you. 'Bout two months ago, 'bout a dozen brothers was hired on at Pacific.'

'That's when Chet started working there, Mr Kovachs,' Ruby Jones said.

Levi Williams gave her a hard stare. 'Who's tellin' this, Ruby, you or me?' She stared right back at him. I looked down at the back of my hands and began scraping the dirt from under my nails. Then Williams looked at me and continued. 'Yeah, Chet was one of the colored guys hired on by Pacific. It was just temporary. The union had got them jobs until the strike was done over at Sears.'

'You mean the warehousemen's strike?' I asked, raising my eyebrows.

'Now, do you know any other strike goin' on over there?' he said with obvious impatience.

'Well, I heard the clerks may go out, too.'

Levi Williams swatted the air with one of his hands. 'I don't know nothin' 'bout that. You want to hear the rest of this or not?' I nodded. 'Like I said, Chet and them boys was over from Sears. They was pickin' up some work for theirselves. Well, I guess 12 new black faces was more than them goddamn peckerwoods could take.'

'Levi Williams!' said Mrs Jones shrilly. 'Don't you use that language in my house. I won't have you cussin'.'

'Well, what would you call them, Ruby? Lord! They done killed your man.'

Ruby Jones looked away from both of us. Her lips trembled. The light from the table lamp next to her revealed her glistening cheeks. She sniffed once and rose from the sofa. 'Excuse me, I've got to look in on the children.' Both Levi Williams and I got to our feet as she left the room.

'She'll be alright,' he said.

I nodded.

'Like I was saying', when Chet and them other black faces showed up at Pacific, things got real angry. You follow me? Yeah, the air got so thick sometimes you could almost cut it with a knife.'

'You think these rowdies were capable of murdering Chet?'

'I'm comin' to that part. At first they didn't pick on none of us special. Sort of spread their mess around even like. Then, 'bout a week ago, they upped and started with Chet.'

'Any particular reason why he was singled out?'

'Not that I'd know. They just started gangin' up on him, like the yellow cowards they is.'

'That rumble at lunch last week. Bill Whitney told me there was some trouble.'

' 'Bout four of them got Chet off by hisself and started pushin' him around an' callin' him all sorts of names. One of the boys seen 'em and rounded up all the brothers and we went over to help Chet. It could'a been a riot, but one of the stewards in the union stepped in and cooled everybody down.'

'You think these cowboys who were picking on Chet maybe got to him later?'

'Mister, I is *sure* of that. As sure as I'm sittin' here talkin'. You see, the day Chet was killed he drew this special assignment to scrape a section of the hull way off where nobody was workin'. When he fell I was one of the first ones there. I saw poor ol' Chet lyin' there all bust up an' I saw somethin' else, too. I could see the rope of that scaffold. It didn't break. It was cut!'

'Are you sure?'

'Mister, I been workin' on ships for a long time. I guess I know when a rope is broke an' when it's cut through.'

'Well, did you show this to anyone else? I mean that's pretty strong evidence.'

'I was takin' care of that poor dead boy. I didn't take no more mind of it until later.'

'What happened?'

'Somebody switched ropes! They took the cut one and changed it for an old worn out rope that looked like it just give out and broke.'

'Did you tell anyone of this?'

'Hell, yes. I told lots of people. Nobody believed me. And the next day, a couple of them good-for-nothing peckerwoods come up to me and told me I'd be a dead nigger if I kept shootin' off my mouth.'

I leaned back in my chair and looked deep into the face

of Levi Williams. That explained his reluctance to talk to me, I thought.

'I know what you're thinkin',' he said. 'Well, I ain't scared of them. I'll meet them anytime they say. No sir, the days when the black man is scared of the white man is coming to an end.'

'Who are these men, Mr Williams?'

Levi Williams looked down at his cigarettes lying on the coffee table. He shook one out and lit it up. A long minute passed. He still said nothing. I repeated the question.

'Man, it could've been one of 15 or 20 guys who cut that rope. Or all of them. Every one of 'em is a dog. A prejudiced dog. But I can't say who did it. It wouldn't be right, lessen I know for sure. I ain't goin' to be the fool who starts a race war. You follow my meanin'?'

In a way, I guess I did. I shifted the conversation to Chet Jones, the man. But Levi Williams was through talking for the night. He told me coldly that he had paid his debt to Ruby Jones and didn't want anything further to do with me. Then, without a word, he got up from the sofa, put on his hat and walked out of the house.

During the next few moments I was back to cleaning my nails. Then Ruby Jones entered the room. She looked around for Levi Williams. She shook her head from side to side as she took a seat on the sofa. 'I suppose he just upped and left?' she said with a trace of anger.

I nodded.

'That Levi Williams is a hard man sometimes, Mr Kovachs.'

'He's just a bit sceptical about me,' I said in polite and understated tones.

'Don't take him too personal, Mr Kovachs. He's had a hard life and it shows sometimes. He lost his daddy when he was a little boy. One of those things the South is famous for.'

I looked down at the floor.

'So, I reckon he's got a right to feel the way he does. I just wish it wasn't all the time like that. God knows black folks got plenty to be hateful about, but we all got to live together in this country. Don't we, Mr. Kovachs?'

'Yes, but I don't know how I'd feel if I was always on the receiving end.'

Before I left I tried to get as much information from Ruby Jones about her husband as I could. She was very co-operative, but didn't provide a whole lot I could work with. When I asked her about Levi Williams's relationship with her husband, she told me Chet and Williams's son – a nineteen-year-old kid named Josh – played baseball together for the Frisco Blues, a team in a statewide Negro league. She said Chet and Josh had grown extremely close during the past season.

I said goodnight to Mrs Jones and told her I would keep on the case for another day or two. She thanked me profusely, even after I told her not to hold out any hope that I could come up with anything.

4.

I would have made an effort to talk directly with Josh Williams the first thing in the morning, but I figured his father would take steps to prevent it. Ruby Jones told me that Levi was extremely protective towards his son and discouraged me from trying to speak to him. She suggested I talk with Rake Holland, the manager of the Blues. William 'Rake' Holland had been a pretty fair ballplayer himself during the '20s and '30s. He played with all the Negro greats – Josh Gibson, Buck Leonard, Satchel Paige, 'Pee Wee' Butts, 'Cool Papa' Bell, names that even white baseball fans like myself had heard about over the years.

Rake Holland was a co-owner of a record store on McAllister Street. I called him shortly after 9 a.m. and told him what I was doing. He said he'd be in the store until noon.

I had to make a stop downtown before going to the Fillmore district record shop. From there I got on to McAllister near the library and drove up the long hill towards the Fillmore. As I drove I had a chance to eyeball the morning. Cumulus clouds, like great heaps of freshly sheared wool, were loping across a hearty alpine-blue sky. The bright October sun warmed my face and the back of my hands. It was the kind of day when *not* to drop what you are doing and go sit on a hill is a misdemeanor. But then, I have broken a lot of laws in my time.

I got to the record store a few minutes before 10 a.m. There was only one person behind the counter. I figured him to be Rake Holland. If I had any doubts, his six foot-plus frame spread out over 150 pounds at the very most gave him away. He knew who I was, too.

'You the fella that just called?' he asked.

'Yeah. Kovachs is the name.'

'I thought so. The only white folks we get in here is musicians and bopsters and you don't look like neither. You said something about Chet and Josh on the phone.'

Before I could speak, a young man came into the store and walked up to the counter. 'Hey, man. You got 'Hamp's Boogie Woogie album?' he asked.

'Over next to that wall. Go on and look. You'll find it. Get you a turntable and play a few licks.'

The young man walked to the record bin.

'Anytime somebody comes in an' wants to buy a record,' Rake said to me, 'I let's 'em play a few licks. That way they know what they's buying and I gets to hear some tunes. I specially dig Hamp.' Rake looked past me to the customer interested in Lionel Hampton. 'Hey there, young fella,' he called. 'Put on *Hey Ba Ba Re Bop*'.' Then, to me, 'Yeah, that Hamp's somethin' else. Him and the cats in his orchestra blew their wigs down in LA last week. They broke all kinds of attendance records at the Million Dollar. Comin' up here next week. I wouldn't miss 'em, if I was you.'

I told him I was more the Billy Eckstine type, but that I would think about going. Then it was down to business. Whereas Levi Williams was as tight-lipped as the lid of a mason jar, Rake Holland loved to talk.

'Yessir,' he said. 'I've been coaching the Blues since '42 and before that I was playing with the best. I played on all the great teams. The Crawfords, Grays, Newak Eagles. All 'cept the Monarchs. And I ain't never seen a couple of ball players like Chet Jones and Josh Williams. Chet was good enough to start on just about any team in the major leagues and young Josh is only a couple years away. Yessir, this here's been the most important year for the

Negro ball player in the whole history of the game. You read the papers. You know how Jackie Robinson tore 'em up this year.'

'Hit .290 or so, didn't he?' I said trying to display my knowledge of the subject.

'.290! Was just a whisker this side of .300! Led the league in stolen bases, too. Did you know that? But that ain't the half of it. He proved he could play with the best of them white boys. And that's just what we been saying all along. Give us a chance. Just give us a chance. Well, Jackie got a chance and look what he done. Hell, we got colored ball players a whole lot better than Jackie Robinson right now.

'I ain't saying the battle's won. They's still plenty of prejudice in major league baseball. But we got our foot in the door. The way I look at it, in another five years there won't be no door left. But happy as I am for our ball players and our people, they's two things I'm truly sorry about. One is that Satch Paige couldn't have played in the majors when he was in his prime. . .' Rake Holland broke off and dropped his eyes. The music of Lionel Hampton filled the space left by his silence. 'And the other,' he said heavily, 'is that Chet Jones ain't never going to get a chance to play. It's a damn shame! That's what it is, mister, a damn shame that an accident had to go and take one of our best young ball players.'

'Some people think Chet Jones's death was no accident,' I dropped in.

Rake Holland recoiled at my words. 'Naw! You don't mean to say?'

'I'm not saying anything. But there is talk.'

Rake shook his head. 'Who'd want to kill Chet?'

'That's what I'd like to know. You knew him as well as anybody, coach. Can you think of anyone who might have had it in for him?'

Rake shook his head again. 'No sir, I can't. Now I ain't

saying Chet was the best-liked boy on the team, because he wasn't. He was a good boy, but when you got as much talent and promise as that, well, it's just natural for some of your team-mates to get jealous. They was a couple of boys on the team that was powerful jealous of Chet. And Josh, too. They was mad, because they knew if anybody was going to make it to the big leagues it would be those two and not them. I got to be honest with you. This integration is a great thing for Negro ballplayers, but it also means it's going to tear up our leagues and set black youngsters against one another, fighting for positions on the white man's teams. See what I mean?'

I did. I asked him if there was anyone connected with the Blues or any other team in the Negro coast league that might have been capable of translating their jealousy into murder. Rake Holland dropped the names of two of Chet Jones's team-mates, but insisted they could not have been capable of murder.

'They didn't like Chet too much,' he said. 'Partly because he was better than they was an' partly because they was older. Nothing smarts an older ball player as much as seeing some youngster come up and take his job away. Like I said, they didn't like Chet, but mainly they just wouldn't have nothing to do with him. Deep down in their hearts, though, I think they knew he was going to be playing in the major leagues, and they was happy. Maybe not for him, but for all the colored ball players coming up.'

'What about Chet's personal life?' I asked, changing tack. 'Was he having trouble with anyone?'

'Not that I'd know. You got to understand. On the field, I knew everything they was to know about the man. I was the one that brought him along. I knew how long it took him to reach first base from the batter's box, how many times out of ten he could peg a strike to the plate from a running catch in center field, when he was going to steal a base and when he wasn't. I knew what he ate, how much he weighed to the ounce, when the muscles in his legs was stiffening up and he wouldn't let on. I knowed all them things and a lot more. But when he left the ball park he was a stranger to me, and everybody else as far as I know. I mean he just wasn't the one to be talking about his personal life. He came to the park to play ball and that's all he talked about.'

'Did you know he was being harassed at work by a gang of toughs?'

'Well sir, that much I did know. But I didn't hear it from him. No sir, Josh told me.'

'Josh Williams?'

'That's the boy. They was real close you know, Chet and Josh. And they was *the* two best prospects west of Kansas City to make the major leagues. I brought both of 'em along, myself. Chet was my number-one boy. My number one. My, my, you should have seen him the way he covered the outfield. You'd swear they was four men playing out there instead of just three. He could run like Jesse Owens, and young Josh wasn't no more than a step behind him. Yessir, Chet reminded me a lot of 'Cool Papa' Bell back when he was in his prime playing for the Crawfords in Pittsburgh. That boy could've hit .300 consistent with any major league team you can name. I think maybe Josh has a little more power, but I'd bet every platter in this here store both them boys could hit 20, 25 homeruns a year up in the majors. And believe me, mister, I ain't one to be bragging on myself just 'cause they's my boys. No sir, what I'm saying is a fact.'

'I'm sorry I never got a chance to see Chet Jones play.'

'It's a damn shame. That's just what it is. A damn cryin' shame. Something like this to happen just when Chet and Josh had a major league tryout coming up.'

'I didn't know that.'

'Mr Veeck of the Cleveland Indians is coming out

himself to look at Chet and Josh. It was all set for the all-star game between the Fellers and the Paiges this weekend. Mr Veeck is going to be right there sitting in the stands giving some boys a good hard looksee. Might even want to take ole Satch back to Cleveland with him.'

I scratched my chin. 'Sure, I read the announcement of the game in the *Examiner*.'

'Ha! An announcement. That's probably all you'll read. They don't cover the colored leagues at all. And the barnstorming tour is, well, I guess it's mighty embarrassing for them.'

'How's that?'

'Well, you know ole Satch takes a group of colored all-stars on a barnstorming tour every year 'bout this time. Hooks up with Bobby Feller's boys. And that man gets him some of the best major leaguers they is. Even brings Jimmy Hegan to catch for him. Well sir, I ain't bragging none, but ol' Satch and his boys like to beat the tar out of them established major leaguers on any given day. They wins maybe two out of three or three out of five from 'em. Ol' Satch has been whipping them for years. And he has whipped Bobby Feller in their pitching duel in the two games they played so far. Last game ol' Satch struck out eight of them white boys in only five innings. Well sir, Bobby Feller done went and challenged ol' Satch to a head-to-head, nine-inning duel, a once-and-for-all showdown to prove which one of them is the best pitcher in baseball. The big game is set for Saturday night down at Seals Stadium. Chet and Josh was going to get a chance to prove theirselves. I got the call from ol' Satch's booking man. He told me to get my two boys ready to play for Satch's all-stars, 'cause Mr Veeck hisself was coming out to take a personal looksee at them. But now . . .' Rake Holland's voice trailed off momentarily. 'But I reckon Josh will still get his chance. He's bound to catch Mr Veeck's eye. You just wait and see.'

I asked the manager of the Blues a few more questions about Chet Jones, but it was all catching up with him. He had a wistful and faraway look in his eye. He seemed to forget he was talking to me. He picked up a record album from the counter, pulled the disc from its sleeve and put it on the turntable near his right elbow. It was Lionel Hampton's *Flying Home*.

Rake looked at me pleadingly. 'No more about Chet right now,' he said. 'I'll just listen to a little Hamp, if you don't mind.' He looked past me and in a moment, Rake Holland, too, was flying home. I don't even think he heard me say goodbye.

5.

It was less than a week ago that the ILWU had put up a mass picket line at the Sears store at Mission and Army Streets. The warehousemen had been striking since early September and the escalation by the ILWU was a response to the Teamsters who were under direct orders from president Dan Tobin to drive through the lines to make their deliveries. *The People's World*, *Militant* and the *Call-Bulletin* all agreed on that much. In fact, The *Call* and her sister dailies in Frisco had run it on page one. Two days after the first mass picket line, the cops escorted the trucks through the line and a bloody brawl followed.

That was a week! The port was shut down by a walking bosses' strike started in LA; the American Federation of Labor convention was grinding away at the Civic Auditorium where the bureaucrats were wringing their hands trying to figure out what to do about John L. Lewis and the Labor Relations Board's non-communist pledge, while they sat and listened to the commander of the American Legion lecture them on the triple spectre of 'fascism-communism-nipponism'. The U.S. consulate in Jerusalem was bombed; Truman was eating stuffed peppers and cheese soufflés at the White House as his contribution to promote 'meatless Tuesdays' and 'poultryless and eggless Thrusdays', all of which was part of a grand campaign to save food and feed Europe. The head of Lever Brothers was running the ad campaign. He came up with pips like 'don't take seconds', 'use left-overs', and 'don't start World War III in your garbage pail'.

And if that wasn't enough for one week, Hans Eisler

was ordered arrested and deported; seventeen year-old heiress Beuhlah Louise Overell and her boyfriend were found not guilty of blowing up the family yacht with Beuhlah's parents on board, and the first of 3,500 bodies of American soldiers killed in the Pacific were sailing through the Golden Gate on their way to their final resting place. The politicians led the city in three days of sober tribute to the 'heroes of the Pacific', as the dailies were calling them.

I try to keep up with my world, but sometimes a guy slips a little. I went down to Local 6 of the ILWU to find out about the strike, the recent confrontations with the police and what, if anything, Chet Jones had to do with them.

Nate Murphy is a steward at ILWU Local 6. He is a big tub-thumper for the ILWU and the Communist Party. He's a decent joe to talk with about broad political questions like the evils of fascism, but when it comes around to the wartime 'no-strike' pledge or criticizing Uncle Joe for little things like wiping out the entire leadership of Lenin's party, he inflates like a rubber innertube and turns purple. And you could just forget a civilized discussion on the Spanish Civil War or the Hitler-Stalin pact. But, like I said, he was agreeable on the broader issues. And that was the basis of our friendship, stormy as it has sometimes been.

The strike was far from over and the hall was jumping with activity when I arrived. Picket signs, a hundred or more, were stacked like cord wood against a far wall. And groups of five to ten men were huddled in various parts of the large hall, caucusing over picketing assignments and strategies. Or so I guessed. I looked around a few minutes trying to spot Murphy. It was just my luck to catch him emerging from one of the offices off the main hall. He was moving swiftly toward the front exit.

'Nate!' I called after him.

He stopped and turned my way. 'Well, Riley Kovachs! Long time no see.'

'Nate. You in a hurry? I need to talk to you.'

'Well, I'm on my way to Sears. I'm a picket captain and my shift starts in 30 minutes. You want to ride over with me? Say, did Ruby Jones ever get in touch with you?'

'So, you're the one!'

'Yeah. The lady needed some help and you're the only private eye I know of this side of the Pinkertons. You are still this side of the Pinkertons, aren't you?'

'Murphy, you ought to go on the radio. Gracie Allen could use a funny man like you.'

'Sorry. I couldn't resist it. Well, are you coming? I've got to shake a leg.'

We walked outside and got into Nate's jalopy. On the way he passed on what he knew about the late Chet Jones.

'What can I tell you? A good man. A family man. A union man. Played semi-pro baseball, too. They say he was a good prospect. Liked to keep to himself, though. The Party tried to bring him round. You know, make friends, struggle over political questions. What a catch he would make, eh? Can you imagine a Jackie Robinson who's a communist?'

'You guys trying to infiltrate baseball now? Is nothing sacred anymore?'

'Ha, ha! Yeah. We're plotting to take over the Cincinnati Reds. That way we won't have to change the name.'

'I guess that's what I like about you, Murphy. Underneath that grim Stalinist exterior is a sense of humor yearning to break free.'

'Did you hear the one about the three guys at the gates of heaven – a fascist, a capitalist and a communist?'

'Oy! I take it all back.'

'No, really. It's a laugh.'

'Some other time. Right now I'm trying to learn everything there is to know about Chet Jones.'

'Pacific will never pay out. The unions will crack them some day, but I'm afraid that doesn't do Ruby Jones much good, does it?'

'We may be talking about something a lot more than death benefits, Nate.'

'Meaning what?'

'Meaning, I know some people who think he was murdered.'

'Murdered!' Nate Murphy's eyes left the road and stared disbelievingly at me. We sailed through a red light at Mission and 16th.

'Maybe,' I said, matter-of-factly. 'It happens, you know. Now what about Chet Jones? Anything you can think of that has happened during the strike, or before, to put him on someone's bump-off list?'

Nate Murphy's eyes returned to the road. He was silent for a moment. 'I don't know,' he said shrugging his shoulders. 'He drew regular picket duty at first, but when he got hired on at Pacific he became a rover.'

'A rover?'

'Yeah. Sort of on call when we needed extra guys. To tell you the truth, Riley, I didn't see him too much. He wasn't in my squad.'

'Well, maybe there's nothing here to go on.'

Nate Murphy snapped his fingers. 'Wait a minute! Chet was on the line the day we had the mass picket to stop the scab deliveries.'

'So?'

'Yeah. He was one of the guys the cops beat up. I didn't see it myself, but one of the guys who was roughed up – a comrade – told me the cops really beat the hell out of him. Like they singled him out special, he said.'

'Because he was a Negro?'

'No, I don't think so. The guy who told me is white and he got clobbered, too. But he said Chet took a real beating. Had to go to the hospital for stitches.'

'Who's the guy who told you this?'

'Name's Rolly Blinn. He's in the Party.'

'Will he talk to me?'

'I don't know. The word's out that you're soft on Trotsky.'

'And you're soft in the head. Look, Murphy, this may be murder we're dealing with. Your man Blinn may know something.'

'Okay! Okay! I'll ask him.'

'When?'

'He should be on the line. Is three minutes soon enough?'

Three minutes later Murphy had parked his car and we were joining the warehousemen's picket line at Sears. Pickets, mostly men from the ILWU and supporting unions, were parading on the sidewalk. The line stretched from the main entrance on Mission, around the corner and down Army Street, turning the corner at Valencia to finish past the parking lot and loading dock.

It was a spirited affair. The pickets were singing some of the traditional union hymns and a man at a loudspeaker was leading chants between songs. Several cars passed and drivers honked their horns as a signal of support. When this happened the pickets cheered and those carrying signs thrust them high into the air.

But the spirit of union brotherhood was not all that was in the air. Thirty or more police with drawn billy clubs standing in formation at the driveway entrances between the picket line and Sears added a heavy note to the scene.

Murphy and I had been in the line a few minutes when he spotted his man. We dropped out of the procession and waited for him to come by. Rejoining the line, Murphy introduced me to Blinn.

The warehouseman was cooperative, but other than describing the beating he and Chet Jones and several others took, he wasn't able to add much to what I already knew about the dead man. He repeated what Murphy had told me about Chet Jones appearing to be singled out for special treatment by the cops. If randomness could be ruled out it was very curious, because the picture of Chet Jones that was emerging was quite the opposite of a vocal militant leader with communist sympathies – characteristics that would provoke many a cop to yank you out of a volley ball game at the family picnic and introduce your head to hard, blunt surfaces just to let you know they were keeping an eye on you. If anything, Chet Jones seemed to make a point of keeping a very low profile.

I was still talking to Rolly Blinn when from 30 yards away a voice called out, 'Here they come!'. The picket line's rhythmic cadence broke off as if the words were some sort of command. In a sense, they were. Two large trucks, escorted on all sides by 30 policemen, were creeping down Valencia Street like the vanguard of a military funeral. They drew even with the entrance to the Sears parking lot and turned slowly – no doubt on their way to make a delivery.

Fifty pickets sat down across the paved entrance and blocked the way. Rolly Blinn and I were just beyond the entrance. The picket line melted and crowded around the trucks hurling insults at both police and strike-breaking drivers. A policeman at the head of the escort phalanx had a megaphone in his hand and ordered the squatting strikers to disperse.

'That's the one!' Rolly Blinn shouted, elbowing me in the side.

'What?' I yelled, trying to hear him above the din.

'That's the cop that creamed Chet!'

I looked back at the cop with the megaphone. He had sergeant's stripes on his uniform. About 35 years old, he had a face like an unpaved road during the rainy season and a look in his eye that suggested he would use a claw hammer to knock the fleas off a tabby kitten. It was a look you couldn't easily forget. I tried to inch my way closer to see if I could get a make on his badge number. But it was no good.

The pickets sat defiantly in the driveway. The police had escorted the lead truck to a point where no more than four feet separated its front tyre from the body of the closest sit-downer. A tense standoff obtained for a few taut minutes. Voices from the picket line, turned angry crowd, yelled themselves hoarse. Muscles in necks became tense and stuck out like the arms of busted umbrellas. Picket signs on broad sticks became potential military equalizers and were shaken furiously in defiance of the scab trucks and their police protectors. The air was hot and thick and angry. Three hundred enraged people packed tightly around the class drama that was unfolding at the driveway entrance.

Then, without a word, the group of policemen escorting the second truck, plus a like number of blue coats positioned inside the human blockade, converged on the barricade of flesh and with clubs drawn, began dragging them out to the street. Some went quietly, while others resisted. Then, like a bolt of lightning, a club crashed down on the head of one of the blockaders. The *thunk* broke through the uproar of hostile cries. For a brief moment, silence obtained and eyes were drawn to the sound – the horrifying sound produced by wood striking human flesh and bone.

The same head took two additional violent blows. And where they connected, bright red blood spurted like water from a broken hydrant. It acted like a signal on the crowd of strikers who surged forward to rescue their injured comrade. Driven by an uncontrollable rage, having witnessed one of their own being beaten into a soft red pulp, they charged through the thin police cordon on a mission of mercy.

The battled was joined. It seemed to last for hours.

Days. But in reality it was over in a matter of minutes. Several policemen were knocked down and beaten with their own clubs. The man whose skull was cracked open was seized by his fellow workers and dragged unconscious to a safe place. Many pickets were knocked to the ground and hammered by well-armed cops. I found myself in the midst of the fray and got off one good connecting right before taking a shot to the kidneys from the business end of a billy club. The same officer rained a combination of blows all aimed at my head. He wasn't lucky enough to connect, but my forearms took a lumping warding off the blows.

The police regained the day after the sit-downers' blockade had been swept away in the melée. Once cleared, the two trucks roared through the opening, hurrying their precious cargo of toasters and bath towels to the haven of the loading dock.

Both sides withdrew to lick their wounds. The picket line regrouped and songs began to fill the air once again. The trucks had gotten through, some heads had been broken and some partisans arrested, but the strike remained. There would be other battles, other days.

I limped over to the place near the corner of Army and Mission where the union had a large urn of coffee. Lighting a Chesterfield, I stood looking at the picket line, the police, the fortress Sears, and trembled. A kind face poured me a cup of coffee and handed me a donut. The coffee was bitter and the sinker well past its prime, but I had other things on my mind.

6.

I left the picket and hopped a bus back to the ILWU hall to pick up my jalopy. From there I headed for another hall. The one on Kearney they call the Hall of Justice. Every corner I turned, both arms and back screeched with pain. It made me think back a few hours to when I was driving up McAllister. Maybe I shouldn't have broken that law. Maybe I should've found that hill to stretch out on and count clouds. That's what my aching body told me I should've done. 'It's not too late,' it seemed to be saying everytime I moved muscle or limb. My nagging mind, however, was telling me to do something else. That's why I was going to the Hall of Justice.

I have always hated the Kearney Street Bastille. Only three kinds of people can be found there – policemen, lawyers and poor folk. That social mix never ceased to work its effect on me.

But I sucked in some air, hitched up my pants and barged into the police squad room. I walked right up to the desk sergeant and slapped my hand on the blotter of his desk to get his attention.

' 'Scuse me, officer, sir,' I said in some put-on accent. I couldn't decide if I wanted to be an Okie or a used car salesman. I ended up sounding an awful lot like a Republican congressman. 'I'm looking for a policeman.'

The desk sergeant, the stereotypical ruddy-faced Irish cop, was reading the sports page. He looked up and smiled. 'Well, now, ain't that nice,' he said sarcastically. 'You come to the right place, buddy. The joint's lousy with 'em.'

I giggled. 'No, sir. I don't mean just any old flatfoot. I'm looking for a particular one. An old service buddy.'

'Well now,' he said humoring me. 'That narrows it down some, don't it? I don't suppose this service buddy would have a name now, would he?'

I looked down at the floor. 'Sergeant. May I call you sergeant?' I didn't wait for an answer. 'I mean it's been awhile since the war. You know, everybody just called him "Bulldog". Sure, he's got a name. Everybody's got a name. But you know how sometimes a nickname sticks and then after awhile you forget the real name?'

'Bulldog?' the sergeant said sceptically. 'There ain't nobody around here by that name. Look, mister, I know we're supposed to be servants of the public, but I'm not so sure that includes you. So why don't you go on and beat it. You're beginning to disturb the peace. Know what I mean?'

'Give me a break, Sarge. Can I call you sarge? Never mind. Look, I'm in town for just a couple of days. Old Bulldog said anytime I blew into Frisco to be sure and look him up. Come on, you know him. He's a sergeant like yourself. Last time I heard he was anyway. About 35. About so tall. Weighs maybe two, two-fifteen. Got a face you wouldn't wish on a bill collector. You know, sort of looks like a bulldog. That's how he got that nickname. I don't know, maybe he's had plastic surgery since the war.

The desk sergeant snapped his fingers. 'Oh! You must mean Watt.'

I hit my forehead with the palm of my hand. 'The very man! Bulldog Watt! Sergeant, you have saved me a heap of embarrassment. I hope this little conversation goes no further than us two. I trust you will keep it, like the French say, "entre nous". I'd hate ol' Bulldog to think I forgot his name.' The sergeant smiled indulgently. I took a perfunctory glance around the room for a moment before returning to the cop behind the desk. 'So, tell me, sergeant. Where can I find Bulld . . . I mean Officer Watt? I don't see him around.'

'Oh, he's on duty. Over at Sears. He pulled strike duty. Actually, he volunteered for it.' The sergeant paused a minute to look hard into my face. 'Say,' he said. 'Were you and Watt in the Marines together?'

'He's told you about it, has he?' I said, sweating quietly inside my clothes, hoping the sergeant wouldn't get wise to the fact that my only contribution to this conversation had been to verbally goose him in the right places.

'I'll say he has,' said the sergeant, smiling and completely at ease. 'You and Bulldog, I mean Watt. Both military police, I bet?'

'Guilty again, sergeant. Say, what's he been telling people?' I said feigning something, but I wasn't sure just what. 'Bulldog always was the one to exaggerate. I'm innocent, sergeant.' I held up my hands and laughed. 'Of 75-80 per cent of everything he's told you.'

The desk sergeant laughed. He snapped his fingers again. 'Say, you're not Spike Boggs, are you?'

I held out my hands like I was about to be handcuffed, saying nothing. But as before, the sergeant jumped the gun.

'Well, I'll be damned!' he said. He stood up and grabbed my hand and gave it a pumping. 'And pardon me all to hell for the way I snapped at you. It's a pleasure to meet up with you, Spike. I guess I've heard just about all there is about you and Watt, from Wake Island to Port Chicago, and then some. Yessir, sure is good to know you.'

I hoped the sergeant didn't catch the bewildered look on my face as I was shaking hands. 'The pleasure is all mine, sergeant,' I said.

The man was really beginning to enjoy himself. Probably had flown a desk stateside during the war and got his jollies listening to other people's war stories. He snapped his fingers again. 'Hey! I'll bet you didn't even know the captain was here?' This time the sergeant did catch the look on my face. He gave a good-natured laugh. 'What, a surprise for the both of you?'

I made my eyes grow large with anticipation. 'You don't mean to stand there and tell me . . .' I paused and waited for the sergeant to help me out.

He was grinning like he had just stolen a freshly baked pie from his grandmother's window sill. 'I sure do! Captain Shultz! He's District Commander.'

'Shultzie? Here?' I gasped trying to look both surprised and pleased.

The desk sergeant was tickled pink. 'I know he'd love to see you, Spike. Here, I'll buzz him.' He reached down the flip the lever on the intercom.

I grabbed his hand as a wave of horror swept my face. 'Sergeant! Please! I want to surprise him.' This time I was the one to snap fingers. 'You know what I bet would get old Shultzie? If I was to go marching into his office dressed like a Frisco cop. You know with a cap pulled way down over my eyes, and just sort of sit on the edge of his desk and smoke a cigarette.'

The desk sergeant covered his giggling mouth like a girl scout who had just witnessed two dogs mating in her front yard. 'I get it,' he said. 'A practical joke.'

'You guessed it. If old spit-and-polish Shultz is still the same, he'll go through the ceiling.'

The sergeant held up his hand. 'He's worse.'

'Well, then, it ought to be a corker.' I looked around the room. 'Just let me borrow a cap and a jacket. That'll do. I don't want to give old Shultzie a heart attack.'

The sergeant laughed and motioned me to follow him to a coat rack on the other side of the room. Before we reached the destination, he turned to me. 'Don't mind me for saying this, Spike, but I had you pictured as a younger man.'

'It's the times, sergeant. Unemployment, mostly. Then there's the bomb to worry about, and Europe ready to go communist. It's aged me a good ten years.'

The sergeant patted me on the back. 'Say no more. I know how it is.'

We reached the coat rack and the sergeant began looking for an officer's jacket that would fit me. 'We always have a couple of spares around here,' he said. 'Boy, I can't wait to see the captain's face when he gets a load of you.'

I held up a hand. 'Sorry, old man . . .'

'But,' he continued, ignoring me, 'I've got to hold down this desk for the rest of the afternoon.'

I put on an officer's cap and jacket that fit me reasonably well. 'I'll hold on to these,' I said, pointing to my own hat and jacket. 'Shultzie will probably want to take me out for a drink. Now, my man, will you kindly point me in the direction of the good captain's office?'

I breathed one of the largest sighs of relief since John Smith saw Pocohantas coming when the sergeant told me Shultz's office was at the other end of the floor. He walked me to the squad room door. I shook his hand and then waved my finger at him. 'And no calling Shultzie and tipping him off.'

He raised a forefinger to his lips. 'Mum's the word.' Then he blinked one eye.

I walked out the squad room door and sauntered down the hall. The minute I turned the first corner, I shed my policeman's garb so fast the friction could have ignited the cloth. I stuffed them in a waste basket near the elevator. Then left the building as fast as my legs would allow.

7.

I spent most of the rest of the afternoon at the Fox theatre on Market Street watching *The Song of the Thin Man*. I needed a good laugh. Munching popcorn, waiting for the adorable Myrna Loy to say cute things like, 'Now, Nickie darling', and trying to piece together what, if anything, that desk sergeant had told me, lasted the better part of two hours. But it wasn't long enough to come up with the combination to that safe which held the secrets that died with Chet Jones. I had my nagging suspicions about a lot of things, but they were just that – nagging suspicions. I planned an evening at home with a hot bath and a pot of grounds to maybe take my mind off my bruised kidneys a bit and help me to noddle this caper through.

The phone was ringing as I stepped into my flat. It was Bill Whitney. 'Riley,' he said. 'You still working on the Chet Jones thing?'

'Working on it, yes. Coming up with anything, no.'

'Well, I got something here maybe you can use.'

'I'm all ears.'

'I only got a minute. I'm on my break. Some guys were sitting at the next table over at the shipyard canteen. Two of them are licensed bigots from way back. You know, the mugs that have been behind a lot of the racial rumblings I was telling you about.

'Yeah, go on.'

'Well, I heard them talking about a meeting they're going to after work today.'

'What kind of meeting?'

'That I don't know. I heard one of them say it was set to

go off at 6 p.m. in a bar on Potrero. A place near Seals Stadium called the Short Stop. Thought you might be interested in checking it out.'

'You want to go with me?'

'Hey, I'm a married man. Besides, they know me. Look, I got to get back to work. Let me know if anything happens.'

Before I could say 'ha!' the phone went dead. A mug like me drops in on a meeting of the Ku Klux Klan or the annual awards banquet of the International Exalted Brotherhood of Thugs and Brawlers. What could happen? But if I wanted to get to the bottom of this thing, I didn't have much choice, did I?

I gave up the hot bath idea, but put a pot on the stove to brew some scorch. Then I called Ruby Jones.

'Oh, Mr Kovachs.' She sounded pleased I had called.

But my call wasn't friendly. 'Mrs Jones,' I said. 'Why didn't you tell me your husband was beaten by the police on the Sears picket line?'

Her voice became soft. 'I, I guess I forgot.'

'Mrs Jones, if I am to do anything for you, I've got to be told everything. I feel that you've been holding out on me.'

'Mr Kovachs, I don't think I like the tone of your voice.'

'Well, that makes two of us, Mrs Jones. Now back to the subject. Why didn't you tell me about the beating Chet took?'

'Is it important?'

'I'm not sure. But I've got to know these things.'

'Mr Kovachs, when a black man gets beat up by the police most white folks couldn't care less. Those that do think he got what was coming to him and maybe even deserved more. Maybe that's why I didn't tell you.'

'Mrs Jones, I'd be lying if I said I know how you feel. It would be even worse for me to say that I sympathize. The way I see it, too many white liberals are so easy with their sympathies for Negroes that it's just another way of saying "go to hell". Now I don't expect you to like me a whole lot, but you're my client and I've got a job to do. And my first rule with clients – all clients – is trust. They've got to trust me. Am I making myself clear, Mrs Jones?'

'Yes, Mr Kovachs, you are. Maybe I was wrong not to tell you more about Chet. But to be honest with you, Chet was a very private man. There are many things about him I will probably never know myself. When he came home all bust up he would only tell me that he was one of the strikers who got hit on the picket line. I tried to find out more, Mr Kovachs, believe me I did. But Chet didn't want to talk about it. And when Chet didn't want to talk about something, wild horses wouldn't make him talk.'

'Well, maybe it doesn't add up to anything. But I'll be frank with you, Mrs Jones. I am running into stone walls trying to find out who, if anybody, had anything to do with his death.'

'Chet was a stone wall, too, in many respects, Mr Kovachs. I was only married to the man for a few years, but he could frustrate a woman, if you know what I mean. He was a proud and private man and he told me more than once that I had to accept that about him if we were going to work out.' She paused and her voice quivered. 'I accepted it because I loved him.'

I grew tense, not knowing what to say in situations when people's emotions are on the table. I tried to steer the conversation in a different direction. 'One last thing, Mrs Jones.'

'Yes?'

'Was Chet in the Marines during the war?'

'No. He was in the Navy.'

'Where was he stationed?'

'I, I don't know exactly.'

'Oh!'

'That was a part of his life he guarded the most. He would never talk about it. I mean, never! I was home in New Orleans when Chet was away. He wrote a few letters, but he never said where he was or what he was doing. I joined him out here the beginning of last year after he had been discharged.'

'Hmm . . . Is there anyone you know of – a fellow sailor – who might know about Chet's wartime duty?'

She hesitated. Only her short, quick breath came over the wire.

'Please, it may be important.'

'Well, there's only one man that I know of. He came over to the house a few times. But he and Chet always picked up and went off somewhere to talk. They never talked around me.' .

'Do you know his name?'

'Washington. Earl Washington. He lives way out in Hunters Point. On Oakdale, I think. I don't know another thing about the man, Mr Kovachs.'

'Thanks, Mrs Jones. And I'm sorry I got rough with you.'

'Mr Kovachs, you were right.'

'Right?'

'About white folks and their sympathy. I'm starting to get a good feeling about you, so don't be spoiling it by feeling sorry for me.'

'Goodnight, Mrs Jones. I'll check with you tomorrow. I hope I'll have something.'

'So do I, Mr Kovachs. Goodbye.'

8.

I drove out to the Short Stop Bar about 5.30 p.m. I walked in, took a stool at the rail and waited for signs of the 'meeting' to materialize. Being in Potrero Hill and near Seals Stadium, the Short Stop was a working man's bar. But not exclusively so. Businessmen in waffle-weave gaberdines, sipping highballs, were not an uncommon sight at the Short Stop. In fact, from the few times I had bent my elbow there I would say it was a watering hole for many of the area's company executives. A place where they waited at shadowed, out-of-the-way tables to rendezvous with fashionable women in 'come-hither' dresses and cloche hats with veils.

I ordered a drink and struck up a conversation with the bartender while waiting for people I didn't know to convene a meeting whose purpose was only an educated guess.

'I'm supposed to meet a guy in here,' I said, taking a sip from my drink. 'Fellow named Spike Boggs. Ever heard of him?'

The bartender had a voice as tired as last year's jokes. His enthusiasm meter was set on snore. 'We get a lot of guys in here named Spike Boggs,' he said, wiping the bar with a soaked rag. He probably wasn't a bad egg. Just tired of answering the same questions for the past 30 years.

'Yeah?' I said. 'Well this Spike Boggs told me there was going to be a meeting here at 6 p.m. and that I could sit in if it was all right with the rest of the guys.'

'Meeting? The only meetings we have in here are some

guys who call themselves The Purity League. Something like that. Yeah, they come in here every couple of weeks or so. In the back there.' The bartender pointed over my shoulder to a couple of tables beyond the pool table. 'I don't see nobody there. You sure it's today?'

'That's what Spike said.'

'I don't know nobody named Spike. A drunk named Duffy runs the group. They're all a bunch of nuts if you ask me. But they don't break the furniture and they drink an ocean of beer. So who am I to complain?'

The bartender said he'd point out Duffy or any of the others when they came in. A few minutes later he came over to me. 'That guy in the pendleton shirt,' he said. 'The one carrying the two pitchers. That's Duffy. The guy with him is his sidekick, but I forget his name.'

I ordered a beer and followed Duffy and his friend to their table. 'Hiya!' I said taking a man-sized swallow of beer while at the same time trying to fight back the grimace produced from the barley slush assaulting my taste buds. I had forgotten just how much I disliked the taste of beer.

'Well, who are you?' the one called Duffy asked suspiciously.

'They call me Spike. Couple guys I know down at Pacific Shipyard said you were holding a meeting here tonight. I'm hoping you're open for new members.'

'What guys at Pacific?' said the other man, a young fellow in his mid-twenties. He was wearing his high school letter jacket, a red and white job that had the name 'Bucky' stitched over a complex heraldic emblem that looked more like a mutt taking a nature break than anything noble that might have been intended. He was the squeaky clean sort. The kind of kid who lettered in everything, was student body president and dated the head cheerleader.

'I don't know,' I said. 'Just a coupla guys I met in a bar

two or three times. I saw them last night. They told me about the meeting. Said I might be welcome.'

Duffy, a large, plain-looking mug with greasy blond hair, looked over at the ex-grad, who shrugged his shoulders. Duffy looked back at me. 'I guess there ain't no harm,' he said. 'I mean we ain't no secret fraternity or nothin'. Sure, why not. As long as you're for keepin' niggers outa baseball.'

I placed my hand across my breast. 'That's a cause I'm ready to fight for, boys.'

Both of them stood and shook my hand and formally introduced themselves. By the time pleasantries were out of the way, five more 'League' members swooped down on the table. Duffy told them about me and no one seemed to care a whit. The main thing on their minds was to get some beer in their stomachs before the meeting started.

By 6.15 p.m. three more had joined the party. One was a first-timer like myself. That made me feel a little easier. Most of the men were young and athletic looking. The majority weren't more than five to ten years out of high school. Duffy was older. My age. As were two or three others. One, a fellow everybody called Myron, ran a hardware store. Duffy worked for the city and at least three others were from Pacific Shipyard. If a person didn't know better, he could have mistaken this hop-soaked gathering for the monthly meeting of the local Kiwanis or Masonic Lodge. But then, for all I knew, maybe it was.

At 6.30 p.m. Duffy stood up and pounded an empty beer pitcher on the table. 'Okay!' he said. 'All you mugs shut up so's we can get the meetin' goin'.' Quiet obtained. 'Okay. There's only one thing on the agenda and that is Saturday night's game. I'll call on Myron to tell us what the plan is.'

Myron stood up amid a spirited round of fake booing and beer glasses pounding the table. Myron was thin and mid-forties. He was wearing a hideous large-checked sport jacket that looked like the test pattern of a television screen. He had a tiny mustache above a pair of thin, straight lips. He looked like a character out of The Great Guildersleeve and gave the impression that he knew everything there was to know about wing-nuts and rubber washers, but not much else.

He smiled and held up his hand to quiet the revelers. 'Thank you, boys,' he said 'Well, as everybody knows, the big game between the Feller and Paige all-stars is Saturday night at Seals Stadium.'

'For chris'sakes, Myron,' interrupted one of the younger men dressed in work clothes. 'Hurry up with it, willya? I gotta take a piss something awful.' Everybody howled with laughter.

'Knowing you, Slater,' said Myron, 'you'll probably go right in your pants.' He wasn't smiling. 'Okay. So it was decided at the last meeting we'd try and get as many people as we could to turn out and sit together.'

'And give the niggers hell!' yelled somebody else from the far end of the table. The rest of the boys whistled and clapped and banged their glasses on the table in agreement.

'That's right,' Myron continued. 'My hardware store is providing two dozen trash can lids and metal ladles to be used for noise, plus the materials to make a banner we can drape over the grandstand fence.'

'Hey, Myron,' interrupted one of the younger guys, who like Duffy's friend Bucky, was wearing his high school letter jacket, 'how 'bout a coupla pounds of bolts so we can throw 'em at the coons?'

At that, Duffy stood up. 'Look, boys,' he said, grinning from ear to ear, 'what you do after the game, on your own, is your business. But this here's a public demonstration. Like a cheering section. Nothing but booing and nigger-baiting. Stuff like that. We don't want no fightin' in the stands. Any knuckle-head who starts something – during the game – will have to deal with me personally. Get it?'

Duffy sat down and Myron had the floor once again. 'That's right, boys. Our job at this game is to let everybody know that we are concerned citizens who are worried about the future of our national pastime. And while we think barnstorming games between the races is okay, we believe if baseball opens the door and lets any more coloreds in, the game will be ruined.'

The boys cheered and pounded the table again. Myron held up his hand. 'Any questions about Saturday night?'

An older man, chewing on a cigar stood up. 'Yeah, I got a question. I heard Bill Veeck is going to be at the game personally to take a look at a couple of our niggers who play on the Frisco Blues. I want to know is that true?'

Myron shrugged his shoulders and looked at Duffy. Duffy stood up. 'I heard that, too. But I also heard that one of the jungle-bunnies he's supposed to take a look at croaked the other week. Maybe the excitement was too much for 'im.' I looked down the table and saw two of the men from Pacific giggle and poke each other in the ribs.

'What about the other one?' The man with the cigar wanted to know. 'He still gettin' a tryout?'

Duffy winked. 'There are ways to discourage all parties from taking this tryout stuff too serious. I can't say no more about it.'

'I think if all this is true,' said one of the men, 'we should find out who this coon is and put the fear of God in 'im.'

The boys banged their glasses and laughed. 'We're looking into a number of possibilities,' said Duffy, cryptically. 'Might be a real good idea if some of you boys was to stay around after the game.' Then he sat down.

Myron was about to field some more questions from the floor when the meeting was joined by two more 'baseball lovers'. 'Conley and Watt!' someone shouted.

'It's about time you two flatfeet showed up. The meeting's just about over.' A few moments of adolescent razzing followed. I even found myself getting into the act and began stamping my feet and banging an ashtray on the table. When I took a closer look at the newcomers, my heart started pounding like the percussion section of a marching band. While not in uniform, there was no mistaking the identity of the two late arrivals. Conley was the desk sergeant whose tongue I had pulled at the Hall of Justice, and Watt was the cop who had bloodied Chet Jones on the Sears picket line.

I pulled my hat down over my eyes and dropped my head into my chest. Conley and Watt were busy trying to catch up with the others in the beer consumption department and took no immediate notice of me.

Myron droned on about the white man's duty to keep baseball 'pure and wholesome' as he put it and to insist everybody write letters to the newspapers as well as the major and minor league club owners to express 'the white man's point of view'. He reminded them of the success such a campaign had had recently in influencing Charles Graham, president of the San Francisco Seals, who had wanted to purchase a Negro ball player named Sam Jethroe, but was forced to admit publicly that he had received too much opposition from the public to go through with it.

I thought he would never stop talking, but some of the beer-drenched bigots at the table, full of hate, and short on attention, began to talk among themselves. And when two 'good ol' boys' got up from the table to take a hike to the powder room, Duffy jumped to his feet, cut Myron off and adjourned the meeting with a reminder for everybody to come early to Saturday's game and to bring their friends.

I rose from the table and tried to soft-shoe my way to the front door. But the bar was dark and the brim of my skimmer was resting on the bridge of my nose which didn't do either my vision or getaway much good. I bumped into Duffy before going 15 feet. He grabbed me by the elbow and asked me how I liked the meeting. As I was begging off, Conley and Watt came over to have a word with Duffy. Although my face was only partly visible, Conley put a make on me.

'Spike!' he said, like we were old friends who went back a long way. 'I didn't know you was here.' He turned to Watts. 'See, Frank, I told you he came by the squad room today. I guess you two have got a lot of old times to talk over, eh?'

Watt was not amused. 'Conley,' he said, 'is this some kind of a joke? That ain't Spike!'

Conley turned to me. He was puzzled. 'Sure it is. Him and me had a long talk this afternoon about you and Captain Shultz and the times you had in the Marines.' A dim light went on in the back porch of his mind. 'Say, Spike. Captain says he never saw you today. What happened? You get lost or something?'

Watt became angry. 'Conley, you idiot. I'm telling you, this guy ain't Spike. I ought'a know my own friends.'

'That's right, sergeant,' I said trying to smear as much banana oil on this little scene as I could. Confusion, in spots like these I thought, can only help. I could smell my goose cooking but I continued smearing. 'Watt ought'a know Spike better than anybody else. It was just a case of mistaken identity. Happens every day, even to the best of us. Believe me.' I raised my left arm to my face and looked at my watch. 'Now, if you gentlemen will excuse me, I really must run.' I started backing towards the front door.

Watt reached past Conley and grabbed my shoulder. 'Not so fast, wise guy. Just who the hell are you?'

'Me? Oh, I'm nobody, really. Just a guy who likes a good laugh.'

'Well, look at me, pal. I'm not laughing.'

'I guess there's just no accounting for taste, is there?'

Watt gave me a small push. 'You ain't gettin' outa here, buddy, 'till I know who you are.'

'Hey! What's going on here?' Duffy demanded to know.

Conley briefed him in a couple of sentences. Duffy scratched his head. 'Hey, Watt,' he said. 'You think maybe this comedian's a spy?'

'I think you got something there, Duff,' said Watt. The three of them – Watt, Duffy and Conley – had me surrounded and I was still more than 20 feet from the door. 'Yeah,' said Watt, scratching his chin, 'come to think of it, I think I've seen this garbage pail somewhere before. How about it, smart guy?'

'You got me there, Watt. I have been somewhere before.' Me and my big mouth. A right arm came from Watt's side and drove a clenched hammer of knuckles into my bread basket. I doubled over.

'You lousy worm,' Watt shouted. 'I don't know what your game is, but I don't like anybody messin' around in my business. Get me?'

I straightened up and held up my hands. 'It was just a bad joke. No harm done. You made your point.' I took a step back toward the door. The look in Watt's eyes told me he wasn't through with me. I could feel Duffy's breath on the back of my neck. There was only one way out of this jam. I took a quick step backward and stomped as hard as I could, hoping to make contact with one of Duffy's feet. A giant yelp let me know I had struck pay dirt. The same instant I let fly with a right that caught Watt square on his cheek.

Then I wheeled and made a break for the door. I remember taking one step, or maybe it was two. Out of the corner of my eye, I saw Duffy hopping around like he was practicing for the finals of the one-legged race. Then I felt something large and hard on the back of my neck. The room began to spin around like the carousel at Playland. I felt myself slip off one of the horses, a pinto I think it was, and fall slowly to the floor. Before the lights were turned out, I couldn't help thinking that this was another jam that I wasn't going to get out of without paying a price. But I tried to see the bright side of it and hoped that the price would only be a couple hours on a cold floor and a headache. It was a possibility.

9.

I heard someone calling my name. The voice was faint and sounded far off like it was coming from the mud flats and on the other side of the Bay. I would have ignored it and gone back to sleep, but the voice kept repeating my name and it was moving closer, too. I still wanted to go back to sleep, but something was stinging my face. I rolled my eyes open and saw a shape bending over me. I could feel the sidewalk beneath me. It was cold and hard. When my eyes focused I saw Bill Whitney. He was slapping my face. I groaned and felt for the lump on the back of my neck. 'How long have I been here?' I said, weakly.

'Just a couple of minutes. When I got home, I got to thinking there might be some trouble here, so I came by to give you some back up.'

'Did we win?'

'I don't think so. You came flying through the front door like a fifty-yard punt just as I was coming in. You nearly knocked me over.'

'Sorry about that, old man. Can you ever forgive me?'

'Are you okay? It looks like they gave you a good going over.'

'You know, Billy boy,' I said regaining some of my strength and getting myself into a sitting position. 'I've been reading this book by Emile Zola. You know, that French writer. It's called *L'Assommoir*. It's still a pretty famous book in France. Only I can't find out what the title means. Who speaks French in this town? It was driving me nuts. Then I'm reading something else about nineteenth century books, and it says *L'Assommoir* translates into something like "the bar where you can get knocked out". I think old Emile must've had this place in mind.'

'Or you. You're still batty.'

'Give me a break, old man, willya? When was the last time you got pounded into cat food by the cops twice in one day? It does give a man pause.'

'Maybe you'd better drop this whole thing. Go home and take a hot bath. Here, let me help you up.'

Bill Whitney held me under the shoulders while my legs pushed off from the sidewalk. When I reached a full upright position my head started pounding like it had been declared a condemned building and the ball and crane had already started tearing it down. I lit a Chesterfield, as if that would do anything. I wobbled a few yards under Whitney's guidance until I got my sea legs.

'That hot bath sounds like a good idea, bub,' I said. 'But I can't drop the case.'

'Are you on to something?'

'Yes old man, that I am. I'm not sure just what, but it looks ugly and stinks like the inside of an old boot.'

'Then Chet Jones was murdered?'

'A hunch and 12 sore ribs would tend to agree with that statement, Billy boy.'

'You going to the cops?'

'Uh, just where do you think I got my ribs barbecued?'

'Sorry, it just slipped out. Arc welding does that to your mind. Well, then, what are you doing to do?'

'I think I'll take that bath.'

'I mean about Jones's murder.'

'There are a lot of details to clear up before I do much of anything.'

'What details? Isn't it clear that some of those boilermakers did him in? The motive was there if what's been going on at Pacific over the last month means anything.'

'Yeah, we start with that. But this thing goes beyond a

bunch of rednecks with welding torches. I mean this thing has been set to music by other forces. Know what I mean?'

'No.'

'Well, neither do I. And now, my friend, if you will point me in the direction of 17th Street where I have tethered my steed, I shall bid you *adieu.*'

'You take the cake, Riley. You know that?'

I tipped my hat, for in my condition, who could argue with that? Bill Whitney turned me around slowly until I was facing in the direction of 17th Street. 'Think you can make it on your own?' he asked in a doubtful tone.

'It'll be easy, my friend. A mere bag o' shells. A mere bag o' shells.' I said steering off down Potrero toward my car.

10.

I soaked in the tub until the mist got so thick I had difficulty breathing and the tips of my fingers puckered up like ten trout grazing for food. I lost track of time, but I must have spent nearly an hour in the soak. I had flipped on the radio before giving myself the boiled crab treatment and 'It Pays To Be Ignorant' which comes on at 7 p.m. was just signing off when I took the plunge. I didn't come out until Brad Runyon had wrapped up the latest 'Fat Man' caper. That was 8.30 p.m., Bulova watch time.

By 9 p.m. I was at the phone with a cup of scorch and a smoke going. I looked up Earl Washington on Oakdale. I found his number in the book and himself at home. He was friendly enough when I told him I was working for Ruby Jones. But when I asked about her late husband's service experience he made like a clam. Other than the fact that they served together in the Navy and served stateside, I learned nothing.

I fiddled with the radio for a while before choosing Philo Vance over the latest puffings from Fulton Lewis. What was Earl Washington keeping from me, I asked the redoubtable radio detective. Did he and Chet Jones get into some kind of trouble? Did this have anything to do with Chet Jones's death? With Watt? Captain Shultz? Was it a racial thing? It was no secret that the Navy had a particularly poor record when it came to race relations during the war. Up until the last year of the war the Navy had a segregated system of training and assignments. Most Negro sailors were either messmen or worked in labor battalions. Much more than that, I didn't know.

Maybe it was the hot bath working its curative powers because it dawned on me that I knew a person who might know the answers to some questions. About the Navy, at least.

Vernell Leggett was a reporter for the *Sun*, the Negro newspaper in town. I met him before the war when I was working on a case down on the waterfront. He was in the longshoremen's union then. He was also active in the NAACP and was just starting out in the newspaper game. I had seen him only once since the war ended, but I remember him telling me he served in the Navy.

He wasn't listed in the telephone book. I would have to try him at the *Sun* in the morning.

I put off until last a call to Levi Williams. I hadn't had time to put together everything I'd heard at the Short Stop, but it didn't sound like those boys were going to be content to sit in the stands and beat on can lids and call people names. If the wink in Duffy's eye meant anything, there was something more in store.

Williams's phone was busy so I rung up Nate Murphy and told him about the Paige-Feller game and the white-sheeted rooting section that was going to be there. I knew he would be interested. The Communist Party had been campaigning to integrate the Pacific Coast League. And the National Maritime Union local here in Frisco had gotten into the act when they issued a public statement that called upon labor and the progressive movement of the city to put pressure on the Seals management to bring up Negro ball players.

Nate was interested. I told him to pass the word along to the baseball fans on the Sears picket line and down at the union hall that they might enjoy themselves at the game. I mean, a duel between Rapid Robert Feller and Satchel Paige to settle the argument over who's the best pitcher in baseball to be fought out right here at Seals Stadium! Who could pass that up?

Twenty minutes later I got through to Levi Williams. He didn't want to talk to me, but I already knew that. Before he had a chance to hang up on me, I told him briefly and quickly, that there was a good chance there would be trouble at tomorrow's game. When he replied that there's always a chance for trouble when whites and Negroes get together, I cut him off and informed him the object of the trouble might very well be his son and that among those doing the objecting were a crowd of slope-browed brutes from the Pacific Shipyard.

He didn't speak for a long minute. Then he told me he would take care of his boy and that it would take the whole state of Mississippi, and then some, to prevent Josh from playing ball and making it to the major leagues. His voice trembled with anger. I knew it wasn't directed at me personally, but I was the only person on the phone, so it was hard not to react. Finally, he told me to stay out of his business and never bother him again. I hung up the phone. I may be many things, but I'm not a buttinsky.

The tunes coming from the Slumber Hour began to get under my skin. I turned off the radio and picked up my copy of *L'Assommoir* and opened it at the page where I had left off more than a week ago. For the next hour I was in Paris.

11.

I called the *Sun* first thing in the morning. Even before my coffee. I was told Vernell Leggett wasn't due in until the afternoon. I pleaded with the voice at the other end of the line for his home phone number, said I was an old buddy and that it was urgent to reach him right away. The receptionist took my number and said she would pass it on to Leggett and if I was an old buddy, like I said, and if it was urgent, like I said, then Mr Leggett would be sure to get in touch with me. Period. End of conversation.

I sat by the phone for almost an hour waiting for him to call. I twiddled my thumbs until they hurt. I drank some grounds and read through the sports pages from last week's newspapers piled next to the stove. I was forced to relive the Browns's agonizing defeat at the hands of the LA Dons last Sunday. Snapped an 11-game winning streak. Beat on a field goal kicked by a guy with no toes!

Time was passing and I was getting nowhere so I decided to take a chance and do something adventurous. I got dressed. My muscles shrieked with pain when I pulled on my undershirt, and tying my shoes was one of the hardest things I've done in years. But nothing was broken and besides the sore kidneys and the golfball on the back of my head, I guess I was pretty lucky. It could have been a lot worse. Sometimes, that thought – it could have been a lot worse – is just about all that keeps me going. I mean being able to walk out of your house on your own two feet after taking a lumping from the bad guys is a way of getting back at them. Lets them know you're still alive and kicking. It must really burn them up.

So, dressed and ready to buy myself a sit-down breakfast at my favorite diner, I walked out into the sun-soaked Frisco morning. But I didn't get far. Two cops in a squad car parked at the curb hopped out and offered to give me a ride downtown. I thanked them, but assured them that unless somebody had pinched my own bucket of bolts, I would take that instead. But they insisted. Said the District Attorney's office wanted to have a chat with me. I was in no position to turn that down.

I had heard of Garth Cane before. He was a hot-shot lawyer who made the headlines a few years back in that Nob Hill murder case that had the whole town talking. He was old San Francisco. Money, Boalt Hall Law School, well connected. A rising star in the Republican party. Or was it the Democratic party? Sometimes it's hard to tell the difference in this town. Anyway, definitely city hall or state legislature material. Currently doing time as Assistant DA.

He was sitting at his desk when I was ushered in by my police escort. He rose to shake my hand. I imagine that for a guy with his ambitions, it must have been a motor reflex.

'Sit down, Mr Kovachs,' he said. It wasn't nasty the way he said it, but I felt like I had been called into the principal's office for running in the halls. He picked up the solitary brown folder lying on his desk and opened it. He rose from his chair and began pacing back and forth across the room.

'Riley Kovachs,' he said, reading from the folder. 'Private Investigator. License number 137597. Since 1931. Arrest warrant issued in 1934 in connection with a waterfront murder. Arrested in '39 in Kingston affair and again last year in the labor dispute in Oakland. A very checkered career, wouldn't you say, Mr Kovachs?'

'Yeah, I've been a bad boy.'

'Three arrests in a dozen years. Not a very good record, Mr Kovachs.'

‘Well, there would’ve been more, but you see, this war came along and sort of got in my way.’

‘You’re being sarcastic with me, Kovachs. I don’t appreciate it.’

‘Say, did you have those two flatfeet drag me down here just so you could read my rap sheet to me? A postcard would have saved the taxpayers a lot of dough.’

‘You don’t seem to understand, Kovachs,’ Cane said, running his fingers through his hair. He returned to his desk and sat down on the edge of it nearest me. ‘You are in a lot of trouble.’

‘Did I forget to register to vote? Silly me. And with the election just around the corner.’

‘It’s a lot worse than that, I’m afraid. Seems you assaulted an off-duty police officer last night.’

‘Well, why didn’t you say so. Sure, I creamed his fist with the back of my head. And then I finished him off by losing consciousness and getting thrown into the street. I’m a brute, you don’t have to tell me.’

‘According to Officer Watt’s report, you verbally accosted him at a place called the Short Stop Bar and when he demanded an apology you struck him.’

‘Add that to Snow White and you’ve got two fairy tales. But in one of them the characters don’t live happily ever after. Is that what you’re about to tell me?’

Cane leaned way over and stuck his face into mine. The smell of his cologne nearly put me under. He was angry, I could tell. Little beads of sweat popped up like dew at his hairline. ‘That’s right, Mr Kovachs. And the big bad wolf is deciding whether to arrest you, pull your license, or both.’

‘Why don’t you just blow my house down.’

‘Any reason why I shouldn’t throw the book at you?’

‘None that you’ll believe.’

‘Tell me. What have you got against Officer Watt? He says you were personally motivated against him. That you told Officer Conley you were a friend of his. And of Captain Shultz, too. Why on earth did you do that?'

'You tell me. You've got my file.'

'Officer Watt seems to think it might have something to do with a case you're working on. Is that right? What case are you working on?'

'Maybe you should ask Watt. He seems to have all the answers.'

"I'm asking you.'

'Don't think I'm not flattered.'

'Well?'

'Well, Mr Cane, does your folder tell you I'm the kind of mug who falls to pieces when Assistant District Attorneys try to shake me down?'

'Don't be a fool, Kovachs. You drop this case – whatever it is – that's caused you and Officer Watt to tangle and you walk out of here the way you came in.'

'And if I don't?'

'I'll suspend your license and prepare assault charges.'

I reached into my coat pocket for my wallet. I opened it and took out my license from the yellowing plastic window and tossed it on his desk. 'Here, roll yourself a smoke with it.'

'I hate to do this, Kovachs.'

I rose from the chair and started walking toward the door. 'Save it for the voters, Cane,' I said out of the corner of my mouth.

'I'll give you 24 hours to change your mind before I file assault charges. My door is always open,' he said. I slammed it behind me. The noise echoed all the way down the hall.

12.

I drove round in circles for about an hour trying to cool off. I yelled at a small boy on a bicycle in Potrero Hill, but didn't really mean it. I finally pulled up at a phone booth in Noe Valley and called Vernell Leggett.

He was surprised to hear from me, but he remembered who I was and that was the important thing. We chatted back and forth for a few minutes to catch up on each other since the war. Then I got down to brass tacks.

'Say, Vernell, I was wondering if you knew anyone stationed at Port Chicago during the war.'

'Sure, lots. Black or white?'

'Black. I'd like to talk with one of the Negro sailors who was there.'

'You're talking to one.'

'You?'

'Yeah. I was there until April of '44. Say, man, what are you driving at?'

'April of '44, you say? You ever know an enlisted man named Chet Jones?'

'Chet Jones? He a brother?'

'Yeah.'

'Chet Jones. Chet Jones. You don't mean the ball player Chet Jones?'

'That's the one.'

'Was he at Port Chicago?'

'That's what I'd like to know.'

'I don't think he was there when I was, but I couldn't say for sure. There were more than 1,000 blacks there during that time. A whole new batch came after I was shipped out. He could've been with them. I heard he got himself killed in an accident last week. The *Sun* carried the story. You working on it, Kovachs?'

'Yeah.'

'You think maybe it was no accident?'

'Yeah.'

'What does Port Chicago have to do with it?'

'I don't know. I'm just following my nose. Hey! I'm the detective. I'm supposed to be asking the questions.'

'You got the instincts of a reporter, my man. Why don't you give up this sneaking around dark alleys and go work for a nice white newspaper like the *Chronicle*?'

'Good idea, but I got this terrible feeling they'd put me at a desk right next to Herb Caen. No thanks. Dark alleys loaded with knuckle-dragging skibos are a whole lot easier to take.'

'Yeah, I see your point. Well, what can I do for you?'

'Vernell, like I said, I'm just playing long shots here, but I might be able to bring them home after I talk with one of the enlisted men who was at Port Chicago in July of '44. Do you know anyone?'

'Sure, I know a couple. Man, what is this all about?'

'It's bad luck to talk about long shots before they come home, but I'll tell you this much. I think Chet Jones may have been stationed at Port Chicago in July of '44.'

'And?'

'He might have been there during the explosion.'

'And the mutiny?'

'Right. I read about it at the time, but a whole lot of the details are hazy.'

'Well, you're talking to the right cat to unhaze you. We got a pretty thick file on the whole thing down at the *Sun*. Why don't you come down and take a look?'

'That'd be a big help. What about some of the enlisted men you know who were stationed there?'

'Sure. Like I said, I know a couple of guys.'

'Will they talk to me?'

'Well, that I don't know. It's still a pretty touchy subject, you know. They'll talk to me, though. Tell you what. Give me a half hour to round one up. I'll get him to meet us at the newspaper. How's that sound?'

'Just what I wanted to hear.'

Vernell Leggett instructed me to sit tight and he would get back to me. Twenty minutes later he called. He'd found a guy who owed him a favor. He had been stationed at Port Chicago in July of '44 when it blew sky high. Leggett said the man would meet us at the *Sun* offices at 11 a.m.

I arrived at the Fillmore district address of the *San Francisco Sun* a little before 10.30 a.m. Vernell Leggett met me at the front door. We exchanged a brief greeting and then he escorted me through the small news room to a store room which housed back issues of the paper. It was small and crowded. Issues of the *Sun* were stacked in deep wood shelves according to date. There was a large desk in the center of the room and two file cabinets in a corner near the only window. Vernell Leggett went over to one of them and pulled open a screechy drawer. He reached out a large file folder choked with yellowing clippings.

'Here it is,' he said, closing the drawer of the cabinet and walking the folder over to the cluttered desk. 'Get yourself a chair.' He motioned to a place on the other side of the filing cabinets where two thin, gray folding chairs sat facing each other.

I pulled one of them next to the desk where Vernell Leggett had already sat down. He opened the file folder and began spreading the clippings in front of him.

'Yeah,' he said, glancing carefully at each clipping before pushing it in my direction, I was there just a couple of months before Chi blew. I knew it would – blow up. Everybody did. You know, some day I'm going to write a book about what happened. What they did to us. You know, name the names. Hit 'em where they live. I got a lot of it locked away in my head, but there's plenty I still don't know. This damn newspaper takes up all my time. But some day.'

I looked quickly from clipping to clipping trying to refresh my memory about the terrible explosion at Port Chicago that killed so many men. And the controversial rebellion of the black seamen that followed. It was all there in front of me in the *Sun* clippings.

Port Chicago, the most important munitions handling facility on the west coast. By July 1944, more than 1,400 enlisted Negro men were stationed there along with a handful of white officers, a couple of hundred civilian workers and a detachment of Marines to guard the base.

Loading ships with bombs and ammunition. That's what Port Chicago was all about. Then on the night of July 17 1944, the *E.A. Bryan*, a liberty ship, literally disappeared in a massive explosion that took place among the 1,780 tons of high explosives in her hold. The explosion took a nearby ship, the *Quinault Victory*, sixteen boxcars, a locomotive, most of the loading docks in the vicinity, and the lives of 320 men. Two hundred of them were Negro munitions handlers. Another 390 were injured, more than half being enlisted Negro men. It was all there in the pages of the *Sun*. It was the worst non-combat disaster of the war.

I was reading an article about the Naval Court of Inquiry, set up four days after the explosion to learn its causes, when the door to the *Sun*'s morgue opened and a man entered.

'Luke!' said Vernell Leggett, looking up from the clippings. 'Don't be bashful. Come on in and sit with us a while.' He made a gesture in the direction of the remaining folding chair located on the other side of the filing cabinet. Luke walked over and picked it up, brought it to the side of the desk opposite me and set it down. He looked at me. 'This the fella wants to talk to me?' he asked Leggett, still looking at me.

'Yeah. Luke, this here's Riley Kovachs. Kovachs, meet Luke Cornell.'

We nodded at each other. Neither of us made an attempt to shake the other's hand. Luke Cornell sat down in the metal folding chair. He wasn't nervous, but it was obvious he wasn't at ease, either. He was a young man – mid-twenties at most – with dark features. Thin and muscular, like an athlete. He reached into his shirt pocket for a smoke, lit it and threw the match on the floor.

Vernell Leggett squinted one eye. He pushed a small metal ashtray on the desk toward him. 'This ain't the *Chronicle*, my man,' he said. 'No hired colored folks to come and clean up after you.' Luke Cornell didn't say anything. Leggett got down to the business at hand. 'We were talking about the explosion at Port Chi and all. You were there weren't you, Luke?'

Cornell looked at me. He took a long drag from his cigarette and knocked the ash into the ashtray. 'Leggett,' he said, looking straight at me. 'What's this all about? Your friend a cop or something?'

Leggett grinned. 'It's cool, Luke. It's cool. Kovachs and me go back before the war. He's no cop. You don't have to worry none about that. He's a private dick and he's working for the widow of a brother named Chet Jones. He thinks. . .'

Luke Cornell shot bolt upright in his chair. 'Chet Jones? Widow? He dead?'

'Then you knew him?' I said.

'Yeah, I knew him. You say he's dead?'

'He was killed in a shipyard accident here in town.'

'Only Kovachs thinks it might be a case of murder,' Leggett added. 'Am I right, Riley?'

I nodded my head. 'And it might have something to do

with the time he served at Port Chicago. That's why I'd like to talk to you.'

Luke Cornell shook his head slowly from side to side. 'Chet Jones dead.' He said he was ready to talk. I was ready to listen.

'Me an' Chet mustered in to Chi together,' he began. ' 'Long with about 300 other guys. Man, there was niggers everywhere, except in charge. I mean it was bad from the git down. A week after we got there, I knowed there'd be trouble. When I went there, I didn't know Chet Jones from his mamma, but after that first week I knowed he was goin' to be in the middle of it. It was just a question of time.'

'How could you tell that?' I asked.

'It don't take long to tell what type of mens you be workin' with. They show theirselves real quick. Chet Jones was the angry type, know what I mean? I mean he didn't mind takin' orders from white men, but he did mind bein' treated like a field nigger. All of us did. No secret about that. But Chet took it more personal than most. I mean he was all the time angry about the way things was run. He didn't go 'round bad-mouthin' the officers to their faces or nothin' like that. But he didn't smile up to 'em, neither. He did only what he felt the rules said he had to do. But don't think them white officers didn't catch on to him. They branded him a trouble maker from the first week. Maybe even before that.'

Vernell Leggett interrupted Luke Cornell. Pushing an article from the *Sun* clipping file across the desk, he said, 'The officers branded anyone who spoke up as trouble makers. Give you some idea what it was like at Chicago when I was there. Luke, you tell him if it changed when you got there.'

Leggett spent the next few minutes giving out the dope on the conditions the Negro sailors worked under at the munitions loading terminal in the north bay. He outlined the process from 'breaking out' the bombs from railroad boxcars to transporting them to the ships, hoisting them by ship booms and lowering them into the holds. He said the work divisions consisted of about 125 men each and they would work the narrow, overcrowded loading pier on seven-hour shifts.

'It was back-breaking work, Kovachs,' he said. 'I'm telling you, back-breaking! You went down in that hold and built yourself out of it stacking bombs and ammo. Am I right, Luke?' Luke nodded. 'We were workhorses, Kovachs. Cheap labor.'

'It's just like he says,' Cornell added. 'Only it got worse when I got there. I mean we heard about how crowded the loading pier was. Everybody was complaining about it. It was just too damn narrow to work. Then in May they widened it. Only thing was, they made us work two ships instead of one. Twice as many men, twice as many bombs. Now you tell me how that's makin' things safer.'

Vernell Leggett stepped in again. 'Down on the docks, before the war, we called what the navy was doing "speed up". No other word for it. Look at it. You had 1,000, maybe 1,500 men loading live ammo and 2,000 pound bombs into ships. They weren't longshoremen. They were kids who didn't know the first thing about ships and even less about explosives. And they were being ordered around by these officers who didn't have any command experience. Hell, they didn't know anything about bombs, either.

'I mean this is a disaster waiting to happen. Am I right? Then in April, right about the time I got shipped out, they started a big speed-up. It was a speed-up on top of a speed-up. They raised the daily tonnage rates for the work divisions and started posting the new rates on the blackboard in the dock office.

'Then those fool officers started the work divisions competing among each other to see who could load the most tonnage during a shift. They treated us like we were boy scouts at summer camp. The work division which loaded the most tonnage would get a movie and a pennant to fly over the barracks. Can you beat that? Damn fool officers whipping us dumb niggers to race against each other in loading live ammo and bombs. They might have just as well sent us to the front with sling shots. Made about the same sense. Hell, at least at the front, a brother could get behind a tree to keep himself from getting killed. What chance did he have throwing live ammo around the hold of a ship?' Leggett laughed sardonically. 'Am I right, brother?'

Luke Cornell smiled. 'Tell it. I mean most of us was scared to death. It took me exactly one shift down in the hold to know that it'll be a lucky nigger that gets out of here alive. Chet and a couple of others started askin' the officers about stuff. Like why was guys who ain't never been trained to run a crane operating the swing booms.'

Leggett interrupted. 'I was right there on the loading pier one day when I saw one of the reps from the ILWU – a guy I knew from before – talking to some of the Navy brass. When he gets through I asked him what's the lowdown. He says the union is offering the Navy to train the boom operators. It's about time, I said. Then he says the Navy gave him the brush off. They're not interested, he tells me. Tells you where the United States Navy stood on the safety issue, doesn't it?'

'Yeah, things was gettin' real bad,' Luke said, lighting up a new cigarette. 'But the brass told us not to worry about anything blowin' up. They said without the detonators in the bombs they were harmless.'

'So you made complaints,' I said. 'Was anything organized?'

'Organized!'

'Did the men talk about doing something together?'

'Yeah, we talked about that. Talked about it a lot.

Some guys even got together and sent a letter to the NAACP. But that was before I got there. Naw, we didn't organize nothin'. I mean how could we? Some of the work gangs pulled slowdowns, but that was about all.'

'After the explosion, what happened?'

Luke Cornell took a big run on his cigarette. A cloud of smoke poured from his mouth and nostrils and rolled over the top of the desk before dissolving. 'Man,' he said, 'those were some scarey times.'

'And Chet Jones. I'd like to know what happened to him.'

It had been more than three years since the disaster at Port Chicago. But to listen to Luke Cornell tell it, it could have been yesterday. 'I was scared.' he said, 'I don't mind sayin' that. Everybody was scared. I mean I lost two of my home boys. They lived right on my street. And I was knowin' a whole lot more that was killed. I mean there you are eatin' chow with 'em one day, sleepin' in the same barracks and all. And the next day they can't even find a little piece of bone to send to their mommas. Everybody in the barracks was jumpy as cats.

'Man, an' we didn't even know what caused that mother to blow. Suppose it could happen again.'

Vernell Leggett waved a clipping like a flag. 'You want to know what caused Port Chicago to go up in a puff of smoke, brother Luke? Well, just for the record, we caused the explosion. That's right. A thousand dumb-assed, don't-know-nothin' colored boys did it. It's all right here in the Judge Advocate's report.'

I took the clipping from him and read a quote from the report of the Judge Advocate who presided over the Naval Court of Inquiry. It stated that the consensus opinion of the Inquiry's witnesses:

> . . . is that the colored enlisted personnel are neither temperamentally nor intellectually capable

of handling high explosives . . . These men could not understand the orders given to them.

I passed the clipping to Luke Cornell. He looked at it a minute and then threw it down on the desk. 'Hell, we could understand the orders, all right. We just thought they was stupid and was like to get somebody killed. And we was right.'

'So, what did the men do when the Navy ordered the survivors back to work?' I asked, trying to focus things.

'We was all shipped over to Mare Island. We knew they was fixin' to make us go back to work and we was still pretty shook up an' all. More'n one home boy cried for his momma at night. That's a fact. Some of the older fellas started sendin' around a piece of paper trying to get all the guys to sign it sayin' we wanted a transfer. Well, I don't have to tell you what come of that. Nothin'!

'Then, 'bout three weeks after the explosion, and we all up at Mare, a ship come in to be loaded. The Second, Fourth an' Eighth Divisions was ordered to go out an' load it. Me an' Chet was in the same battalion. More'n 300 men total. Well, we just said to hell with that, go load your damn ship your ownselves. That's what we said.'

'That's when everybody got arrested, wasn't it, Luke?' said Vernell Leggett.

'Yeah. Some of the men got scared and went to work. But only about 70 of them. The rest of us was arrested and put on a barge out in the Bay an' kept there for three days under Marine guard.

'Man, that's when they really came down on us. These big-time white officers tellin' us we no good raggedy-assed mutineers and that we was all goin' to be shot. And them Marines! They was the worst. Callin' us all kind of names. Butt-strokin' us with their rifles for no reason. Man, they was bad. There was a big fight between them and some of the fellas in the chow hall. Ol' Chet an' me was right in the middle of the damn thing.'

Luke Cornell paused to light another cigarette. I pulled a Chesterfield from my shirt pocket and got it going. I popped a lifesaver into my mouth to sweeten the taste, and asked Luke to tell me about the fight that took place on the prison barge.

'Well, I don't exactly know what started it, but this big ugly Marine come by an' said somethin' to Chet. I couldn't hear what he said, but Chet must a not liked it, 'cause the next thing I know, Chet done popped him on his jaw and the fight was on. Chet got hurt pretty bad an' I lost a tooth when one of the guards cold-cocked me and I fell on the deck.'

'This Marine who worked over Chet. Do you know his name?'

'Naw. I never seen him before. He was a big, ugly mother, I can tell you that. He was a insult to his momma he was so ugly. And mean!'

'You never knew his name, though?'

'Naw. But about a year ago I got stopped on the Bayshore for speedin'. An' who do you think pulls me over?'

'Same guy, right?'

'You guessed it. This ugly dog Marine is now a San Francisco cop. I recognized him all right.'

'What happened after the fight on the barge?'

'Well, the next day they takes us off the barge and marches us over to the baseball field at Mare. They got every Marine on the base guardin' us with their bayonets fixed. You hear me? They got their bayonets fixed! Then this big old jowled Admiral come ridin' up in a jeep. Admiral Wright. An' straight off he starts hollerin' at us like we was a bunch'a runaway field slaves. Tellin' us we a bunch'a yellow cowards and that what we doin' is mutiny an' we sure be facin' a firin' squad if we keep it up.

'Then he gets back in his jeep an' cuts out. Man, that old

cat put the scare in us. I mean when a Admiral tells you you goin' to get shot, they's a good chance you goin' to get shot.

'The next thing I know after that is the division officers make up two groups an' tell us to pick one an' fall in. One group is for guys who is goin' to obey orders an' go back to the ships, an' the other group is for those who still ain't goin' to follow orders to load no ships with live ammo. Man, it was a lowdown thing they done tryin' to split us up like that. A lot of the men didn't know which group to go into. Then I remember Chet jumpin' up an' shoutin' for all of us to stick together an' fall into the group that wasn't goin' to obey orders. I gotta hand it to the man, he had guts. I mean them Marines had their guns pointed right at us and was just itchin' to kill theirselves some niggers.

'But Chet, he kept on a talkin'. He was gettin' some of the fellas to switch outa the group that was for obeying' orders. Then I seen the Marine commander, some shave-headed Nazi-named son-of-a-gun, give the order to the guards to shut Chet up. That same ugly dog leatherneck who had whipped on him the day before goes over an' butt-strokes him with his rifle. They was nearly another riot, but they had guns an' we didn't. We ain't no crazy colored folks like y'all thinks.

'So when it's all over, there be 50 in the refusin' group an' 200 in the group that was decidin' to go an' load. I ain't no damn hero, so I sticks with the group that is willin' to work the ammo ships. I'd a rather stuck to the other group, but I knew those boys was in for more trouble than I could handle.

'But it didn't do no good to be with the obeyin' group. No good at all. Instead of puttin' us back to work like we thought, they sent us to Camp Shoemaker and throwed us in solitary. Then they made us say things about the guys in the other group that was all lies. And when that was over, they gave us summary court martials. We was tricked, in other words. Just plain-out tricked.'

'Do you know what happened to Chet?' I asked.

'Well, we was in solitary for a good long time, but I heard later those guys who fell in the refusin' group was brought to trial for mutiny. Wasn't much of a trial, the way I heard it. They was all convicted. Funny thing, though.'

'Yeah, what was that?' I asked, taking out another Chesterfield from my pack. I offered Luke Cornell a smoke. He waved his hand no.

'Chet wasn't in that group that got sent up for mutiny.'

'Oh?' I said, lighting my tobacco and throwing the match in Vernell Leggett's ashtray.

'Yeah. I read all about it after I got out of the brig. I saw a list of names, but he wasn't on it. An' since everybody who was in on the thing got scattered every whichway, they was no way I could find out what happend to him.'

'Do you have any theories?'

'Well, at first, I thought they killed him. You know, for bein' a ring leader an' all. Yes sir, I thought they murdered that poor boy. But then, 'bout a year ago, I seen his name in the papers. He was playin' ball in the Negro league.'

'What did you make of it when you found out he was alive?'

'Well, I don't like to say nothin' bad against nobody, specially a fella like Chet, but I figured maybe the Navy got to him.'

'Got to him?'

'You know, like maybe they let him off easy in trade for some information about the others. Somethin' like that. I ain't got no evidence or nothin', an' even if it's true, I don't blame the man. I mean the brass had us running' so scared a man was like to do anything to keep from crackin' up.

'After I read 'bout Chet in the papers I tried to see him.

Found out where the Blues was playin' – that was his team and went to the game. I wanted to know what happened to the man. But when I saw him he got real mad an' wouldn't talk none about it. No way he would talk about it. Kinda made me think I was right about what I was thinkin'. But I don't know for sure one way or the other. An' like I said, I couldn't blame him none. No sir. The man had guts an' he did what he had to do. We all did. It was a hard time. A real hard time.'

Luke Cornell stopped talking. He looked over my head. I don't think anything particular caught his eye, he just didn't want to look at me. Or Vernell Leggett either. He was concentrating on other things more important to him. Like that time after July 17 1944 – those few terror-filled months that would probably live with him and the other men for a long time. Maybe forever.

Vernell Leggett broke the silence. 'Here's a story on the sentencing,' he said, holding out a *Sun* clipping. 'Take a look at it, Kovachs. These 50 boys sent away for refusing to get themselves blown to smithereens. Some crime, eh?'

I looked at the article. Ten of the 50 'mutineers' were sentenced to 15 years hard labor. The rest received sentences from 5 to 12 years. All of them were dishonorably discharged.

'But don't be thinking America doesn't have a heart,' said Leggett, sarcastically. He spread out four or five clippings in front of him and told me how the Negro press and the NAACP mounted a campaign to free the convicted men. He explained how Thurgood Marshall took their case and pressed it with the Secretary of the Navy. The case drew national attention.

'It took a while,' he said, pointing to one of the articles in front of him. 'But look here. In January 1946, Forrestal released the men. Sent them overseas for what the Navy called rehabilitation. I'd call it exile, but we did get them off. And called the Navy's hand on segregation, too.

Forced it to end segregated training camps and some other things.' Leggett turned to Luke Cornell, who was still gazing at the wall. 'What do you think, Luke? Anything good come out of that mess?'

Luke lowered his eyes and focused them on the reporter. He looked at him a long minute before speaking. 'I can't really say. Some says a little good comes from everything. Even the worst things. The men got off and that was good. But they paid for it. The Navy made all of us eat a lot'a dirt. You know what I'm talkin' about? They never treated us like men. That's somethin' I'll never forget, no matter how things change from now on. I just know that I gotta live with what happened. That explosion. My buddies dyin' an' all that fuss that come after. Maybe sometime it'll die down in my brain, but for now it means I don't get too many good nights' sleep. A thing like that sticks with a man for a long time.'

Vernell Leggett nodded his head in agreement. He hadn't intended to discount any of the pain Luke Cornell and the others must still carry with them. Total silence obtained for the next few minutes. Everything had been said and I could tell that it had taken a lot out of him to relive those days. He lit one more cigarette and then got to his feet. He walked to the door. Vernell Leggett walked with him. They exchanged a few words and Luke Cornell left.

Leggett returned to the desk and sat on the corner of it across from me. 'Yessir,' he said, in a soft, almost distant voice. 'Someday, I'm going to put all this down in a book. Tell it from the enlisted man's point of view. The Negro sailors who went through it. I know Luke and the others got a whole lot more to say. A whole lot more.'

I nodded and thanked him for getting Luke Cornell to speak to me. I got up to leave.

'Did it help the case any?' Vernell asked.

'Yeah. A few more of the pieces have found their way

into the picture. I'll know more by tomorrow night.'

'Tomorrow night?'

'After the ball game at Seals Stadium.'

'You mean the Feller-Paige game?'

'Yeah.'

'I'm not even going to ask how it fits in.'

'I probably couldn't tell you anyway, Vernell. Not for sure.'

'Hey, I'm covering the game for the *Sun*. Filling in for the sports reporter. He's out sick. Want to go together? I can get you in on my press pass.'

'That'd be swell, old man.'

'Yeah, I'm doing an interview with Satchel before the game. You can sit in on it if you want. Just be in the locker room by 6.30 p.m.'

I thanked him for the offer and assured him I would be there. Then I told him briefly about the Pacific Coast Purity League shindig on tap and suggested it might be a good idea to pass the word along to his baseball fan buddies down on the docks. 'Going to be a hell of a game,' I said, winking at him.

We shook hands and I left him in the *Sun* morgue. He said he wanted to go over the Port Chicago clippings some more. It was 2.30 p.m.

13.

It was a sunny day in the Fillmore. Low 70s. Warm. The mid-afternoon sun shone the color of old gold, a color you can find on coffee tables and lamps in Sea Cliff mansions.

Twenty minutes later I reached the ocean. The Cliff House, to be exact. The sun, the sky and most of the people had disappeared. Swallowed by a fog the color of wet cement. And I had come to take in the sights. I had some time to kill and I planned to hike from the Cliff House, along the craggy bluffs to the Legion of Honor. I figured I could sort my thoughts out along the way. I hoped the fog was not some kind of omen.

I bought myself a 'batter pup' at the snack food stand next to the Cliff House, then went downstairs to fool around in the Musée Mécanique. I stopped on the lower landing to take a gander at Seal Rock, and put a penny in the telescope to get a closer look at the hundreds of barking flippers who have manhattanized the big rock just beyond the beach. After a minute the telescope went dark and I carried on to the museum.

It's not really a museum. It's more a turn-of-the-century mechanical games and peep show. You know, wooden villages with puppets rotating and moving about, stereoptican slides of the 1913 Panama Exposition that took place right here in Frisco. Things like that. And there are a few old-time games that are still in working order. I like to come down and play the baseball game. It's a ball and lever job. A mechanical pitcher rolls a steel ball and you operate the bat by pressing a button. The pitcher can throw curves and change speeds on you so it is not as simple as it sounds. I'm a sucker for a curve ball, but I've been getting better the last few times I've played.

I walked up, took out a handful of change and placed it on the glass case. I put a nickel in the slot and prepared to match wits with the mechanism controlling the balls. The first three balls rolled past me like I was standing in another part of town. Then I connected for a single, then a double. I was getting the rhythm of the thing when the pitcher threw me a changeup and I missed it by a mile.

I reached for another nickel, but my hand missed and knocked the change to the floor. As I bent to pick it up, I could see the reflection of the Golden Gate and the Marin County coast in the glass case. But that wasn't all I could see. Standing in the corner of the doorway was a man, a Negro man, and he had a gun in his hand. Reflections can play funny tricks on you, but it looked like the gun was pointing at me. I decided it was no time to take chances and dived under the baseball game just as I heard the gun go off. The glass case sprayed shattered glass all over me.

Some of the half-dozen or so visitors in the museum screamed and I saw people ducking for cover. I rolled out and scrambled to my feet. The man at the door had a partner who was also packing lead. I raced deeper into the museum looking for the closest thing that would provide cover. I heard another shot, and then another. I lunged for the protective safety of the dancing elves nickelodeon.

I would have reached inside my coat for my blower, but since Cane pulled my license I had to ditch the gun or risk being picked up by anyone with a badge. But then I probably wouldn't have been packing it anyway. It just didn't occur to me that I would need a gun to look at the seals and play a few innings of mechanical baseball. Silly me.

I peered out from behind the nickelodeon and saw the two shooters. There were standing just inside the doorway looking extremely nervous. They looked reluctant to come after me, if for no other reason than there was no rear exit to the museum. They were smart enough to know that the sound of their shots were bound to bring the cops pronto. After all, the Cliff House is a tourist attraction.

'Let's scram!' one of the assassins said, backing toward the door.

'You're a dead man, Kovachs,' the other shouted as he took one last look around before retreating.

Everyone inside the museum stayed covered and quiet for several minutes after the men left. Then the cops came. I answered a few questions put to me by the officer in charge. Then I left quietly. I didn't feel like challenging any more curve balls.

I didn't go up the stairs to the street, however. There seemed to be a good chance those two bulleteers had reloaded their hardware and were laying for me.

I scrambled over some very sharp rocks and down to the footpath that took me to the Sutro Baths. It's a place that looks like it was designed by a guy who was getting paid by the square foot. A giant structure with six swimming pools, a forest of tropical palms and loads of galleries and promenades. There's always a couple of thousand people swimming, promenading and just hanging out on any given day of the week. An ideal place to hide.

I took a table behind a palm tree and sipped a coffee for the better part of an hour waiting for the coast to clear. Figuratively speaking. When I felt safe – as safe as I could with the cops, the assistant DA and two guys I didn't even know just waiting to have another go at me – I left the Sutro Baths.

The fog was as thick as Marlene Dietrich's accent as I scrambled up the small bluff behind the baths. I hit the bush a minute later and began the 30-minute trek over sand, beach shrubs and crumbling hillsides.

Foghorns droned lazily in the distance sounding like bored tubas. The gray steam collected on my lip and shoe tops. A chill went through my body. It was only 3.30 p.m. but it could have been midnight. Visibility was the nearest tree. But, in a way, this was the best kind of weather to put on the old thinking cap. There were no visual distractions and that's a fact. No amateurs with guns, either.

Some of it was coming together. The Chet Jones case, that is. Most likely, Levi Williams was right. The ropes to the scaffolding had been cut by one of the hard-core bigots at the shipyard. The fact that Chet Jones was a top-notch baseball player on his way to the big leagues provided at least one motive to kill him. 'Baseball's a white man's game', as they are fond of saying at the Short Stop. But bigots always have motives to do evil things. You don't have to provide them with one.

However, since even in a group they have the collective intelligence of a box of cornflakes, they must have been ignited. Given a shove. Set in motion. That's where the dead man's war-time service came in. From what Luke Cornell told me, it wasn't hard to figure out that Chet and sergeant Watt tangled during the Port Chicago/Mare Island 'mutiny'. They had bloody run-ins at least twice.

The way I had it figured, Chet Jones locked that part of his past away in an iron strong box after the war. Whether or not Luke Cornell's theory about him was correct, I could see why Chet would want to keep that episode from reaching the wrong ears. Especially employers, creditors and the like. And Watt. He left the service after the war and joined the Frisco police force. He must have put Chet Jones and Mare Island behind him, too, until that day when the two of them came face-to-face on the picket line at Sears. At that point the old hatred flared and Watt, not content with beating the stuffing out of him on that Mission district street corner, must have arranged, through his beer-drinking cronies of the Purity League, the murder of Chet Jones.

But there remained some questions that had yet to be answered. I could think of at least four. First, did the murder of Chet Jones stop at Sergeant Watt or did it go higher up the ladder? Second, why did the DA pull my ticket if it didn't? Third, who were those colored guys with the flame throwers and how did they fit into the picture? And lastly, what were Duffy and his nightriders for the national pastime planning for tomorrow's game and what did they have in store for young Josh Williams? I guess that's five questions. Five unanswered questions. Not bad considering it seemed like it was only a few hours ago I was in the Chat 'n Chew drinking coffee and minding my own business. At that point I hadn't got my kidneys relocated and no one was shooting at me. Those were the days.

I like to think it was the cold and the fog that gave me a shiver. A clammy wetness soaked through my clothes, but I didn't mind. I like the fog. It's mysterious, silent and sneaky. And it's constantly moving and changing its appearance. A lot like the old game of life itself, as I'd bet cash money some poet has written somewhere.

I walked across the fairway of the Lincoln Park Golf Course and up the bank to the road that runs behind the Legion of Honor Museum. The fog was thinner and I could make out the statue of El Cid astride his horse standing in the middle of the museum's northwest lawn.

I walked up the stone path between El Cid and the colonnade porch of the museum. I stopped and looked in the same direction El Cid was looking. The fog was breaking up. That is, it was compacting. A dense bridal-white train of steam was coasting through the Golden Gate. Above the fog was the top of the orangy sumac-colored towers of the bridge and the fuzzy brown floating ridge of the Coast Mountains across the water in Marin

County. And above that were thin strips of a vague, white, cloudy sky. Foghorns with different timbred voices continued to call out like tubas tuning up for a concert.

I walked past the Rodin cast of the Thinker and into the museum. It's a classy joint, the museum, built some 25 years ago with a sugar baron's dough. It's a replica of the Legion of Honor in Paris. Both the building and the grounds of the Frisco edition are the rooster's boots as far as I'm concerned. That's why I like to go there. The art inside is another story. Mostly seventeenth and eighteenth century French art. In my book, from what I know, with the exception of some landscape painters, most of that period was downtown dullsville, artistically speaking. The Legion's galleries are chocked full of squirely aristocrats in powdered wigs and nymphs with powdered breasts. Save for a couple of Fragonards and a Watteau that's not too hard on the eyes, you can keep it all. Your Le Bruns, Le Nains, Bouchers. You name them.

But like I said, it's the building itself and the grounds and especially the coastal hike up to it from the Cliff House that charges my battery. So, every six weeks or so, I find myself standing in front of French paintings and sculptures. Over the year, I guess, I've become something of an amateur egghead on the subject. But then being in the know about art is probably a whole lot easier than being in the know about books or classical music. I mean in literature, you have to read long books and then when you finish them, you have to read other long books that tell you what you have read. The same for music. You have to read books that tell you what the music is all about or how to recognize a scherzo. Things like that. And all that takes time.

With art, you just stand in front of a painting for about half a minute, read the little tag underneath it and try to remember it. And unlike books and classical music, most art museums are laid out with all the paintings and sculpture put in galleries in chronological order. What could be simpler? You go to the museum every six weeks or so, flip through an occasional book on art history and presto you're an expert and can talk about the Regency Period like a connoisseur. Or discourse on the debate between the Classicists and the Romantics, if the subject ever comes up, which in my line of work is about as often as you would expect. In my world, art is more likely to be a 200-pound face-breaker waiting down some dark alley to do a knuckle polka on my kidneys. But you never know.

I walked briskly through the seventeenth and eighteenth century galleries, into the other room, stopping briefly to pay my how-do-you-dos to 'The Burghers of Calais' and a Pissarro I'm quite fond of before heading for the one painting that brings me back time and time again.

On the way, I stopped for a moment to glim an insipid Boucher, just to reassure myself I hadn't been giving him a bum rap all these years. Two well-dressed women were standing in front of me. One or both was wearing perfume strong enough to knock over a bank. I turned away and reeled into the seventeenth century landscape room.

My painting hangs in a far corner of the gallery across from a Claude Lorrain. It was painted by a man named Patel, a mug who isn't in any of the books. I know because I've looked. Sometimes you can find his dates, but not much else. Once, I looked him up in an old art encyclopedia. I found out that his father was also an obscure painter. Of the son, the book said, 'less is known than concerning his father with whom he is often confounded'. But he must have been somebody if the Legion has one of his paintings on its walls.

'The Month of October 1699'. That's the name of it. I walked up and planted my feet squarely in front of it for the tenth or twentieth time since I discovered it a number of years back. It's the kind of picture that you want to climb right into. You know, back to 1699. I don't know why it makes me feel like that. It just does.

Maybe it's the sunset. The left half of the painting is a rich, creamy peach, orange and lavender, while on the right the sky is still crystal blue and full of clouds. Or maybe it's the mountains in the distance. There are three buttes that have turned a purple slate in the twilight.

Then, maybe it's the village in the foreground that curls an inviting finger at me. Or the little settlement in the hills above the village. Two huge chestnut trees on earthy mounds dominate the center of the painting as well as the settlement. On the left, under the trees, is a small garden being minded by two peasant women. In the lower right, darkness is falling on several plain stone houses. People are on the road in front of them returning from their day's labor.

But maybe it's not 1699 or the month of October that get to me. I think it's the time of day the painter captured. Twilight, where 'time stands still for a minute', some writer once wrote, 'where the day pauses to examine itself'. Where the gold of the day meets the blue of the night. Bing Crosby said that.

Yeah, it's the twilight. Dusk. When time does stand still for just a minute. The day trapped in amber. A private time. The quiet time of each day when people are given the chance to lament the passing of the sun and blue skies or maybe heave a big sigh of thanks that another period of back-breaking, life-dulling labor has taken time out.

I left the museum and my painting. It was 5.30 p.m. Twilight. It was the month of October, 1947. I had the same feeling the painting always gave me. Only I didn't have the urge to climb into another dimension. I was already in it.

14.

It was finally dark and I felt a whole lot safer in this 'cool, gray city of love,' as some poet whose name I forget referred to Frisco. Ha! That's a laugh. I hopped a bus from the museum that took me back to the Cliff House where I picked up my car. I drove out to Ruby Jones's apartment for some answers.

She opened the door, but not very far. It was clear that I wasn't to be invited in.

'Oh, Mr Kovachs,' she sounded surprised. 'I was trying to call you.'

'Strange things have been happening to me, Mrs Jones. I need to talk to you.'

Her eyes darted away from me and followed a car speeding down the street. 'I have company at the moment, Mr Kovachs. I wanted to tell you everything is all right. I won't be needing your help anymore.'

'All right? Mrs Jones, the DA suspended my license and two men just tried to kill me down at the Cliff House. Everything is not all right.'

Ruby Jones's face registered first shock, then horror, then nothing. 'I'm sorry, Mr Kovachs, but you see the shipyard has decided to pay me some money. It isn't much, but it's better than nothing. So, please, if you will just tell me how much I owe you.'

'You owe me an explanation, Mrs Jones. I'm pretty sure your husband was murdered. Whatever you got from Pacific is a buy-off to sweep everything under the rug.'

Tears began spilling down Ruby Jones's cheeks. Her watery eyes focused on the floor in front of her. 'Please,

Mr Kovachs,' she said in a pleading voice. 'It's over. I got my money. It's the best I can do so you must forget it.'

'Would your husband have wanted me to forget it, Mrs Jones?'

Her tears turned to sobs. 'I have to get back to my company now. I will send you some money in the morning.' She closed the door in my face. I could hear her sobbing as she walked down the hall. I lit a cigarette and returned to my car.

They got to her all right. Somebody wanted this thing hushed up. But who? Cane, to protect a pyschopathic cop? Levi Williams, to protect his son and prevent a race war on the docks? Pacific Shipyard, to prevent a potential investigation into their 'safety conditions'? Duffy's gang, to protect the murderer in their ranks? Who?

And who among them would want to send me to boothill? Seemed like they all would have their reasons. But there was another angle. Something Rake Holland said about a couple of Chet Jones's team-mates made me think it was time to pay the coach another visit.

It was past 7 p.m. when I got to the McAllister Street record store. The place was dark and the 'closed' sign was up. I peered at it to see if there was a phone number I could call. Funny, I thought, that Rake Holland's shop was closed. It said it was open until 8 p.m. I banged on the door. Maybe Rake had closed up early and was in a back room spinning some platters for his private enjoyment. So I banged loud.

Not drawing any response, I turned to walk away. I hadn't taken a step when I heard a sound coming from inside the store. A low, muffled sound. Like a moan, maybe. I pressed my face to the glass door. I couldn't see a thing, but I heard another moan. This time it was louder.

I banged on the door again and called out Rake Holland's name. When I heard a third groan I took a little gadget from my pocket burglars sometimes use to pick locks with. Mine was subtly different in that I'm not a burglar. I inserted it in the lock and gave it a turn. The door was easy.

I groped my way into the darkened store running my hand along the wall looking for a light switch. I found one and flipped it on. Another groan directed me to Rake Holland. He was crumpled up under a record bin in the middle of the store. I rushed to him.

'Rake! Are you all right?' I asked stupidly. I mean when you see a person sprawled on the floor looking like a stack of old newspapers someone's kicked over, blood all over their face, it should be clear they're not all right. But then that's just another example of the language's shortcomings, isn't it?

Rake Holland was conscious, but barely. I took out my handkerchief to wipe the blood from the side of his face, but it had dried and become caked. He must have been lying there for some time.

'Rake, it's me. The fella you talked to about Chet Jones. Remember?'

'His eyes were beginning to focus. 'Oh, what time is it?' he said.

'I don't know. After 7 p.m. What happened here?'

'Who are you, mister? You the police?'

'No. Kovachs. Remember? I talked to you about Chet Jones. I'm working for his widow.'

'Oh, yeah, I remember. Help me up, willya. This floor is giving me a chill.'

I helped him to a chair next to the counter. He wobbled like a bent wheel for a moment then seemed to regain his strength.

'What happened?' I asked again. 'Did someone rob you?'

'Rob me?' he repeated like I had just invented the term. 'Naw.' He rubbed the side of his head slowly. The expression on his face indicated it was all coming back to him. 'They hit me. Yessir, those boys done laid out the old coach.'

Rake Holland slowly got to his feet. I went over to steady him but he pushed my arm away. 'I'm all right now,' he said, walking slowly over to one of the turntables. He turned on the juice and began looking through one of the record bins. 'Now where's that Hamp I was playing today?'

'Who hit you, Rake?' I asked trying to get back on the right track.

'Let me find this Hamp. Playing a couple of sides helps my head.' He put a record on the turntable and lowered the needle on it. He turned and walked back to his chair. He was rubbing his head as he sat down.

'Damn! Feels like they used a tyre iron. It's a miracle they didn't bust my coconut wide open.'

'Who are they?'

'Couple of boys from the team.' He almost stopped before he finished his sentence. 'Say, you ain't seen 'em, has you? I tried to stop 'em. Talk some sense into their fool heads. But you can see where that got me.'

'If we're talking about the same thing, it almost got me a front row seat at my own funeral.'

Rake Holland shook his head. 'I tried to stop 'em. Told 'em they was wrong about you, but they wouldn't listen.'

I then filled him in with the details on the shooting at the Cliff House. I didn't have to describe the pistoleros. Rake knew they were his boys.

'Mmm, mmm, mmm,' he said shaking his head from side to side. 'They isn't bad boys, mister. Some mens told 'em lies on you. Told 'em you was mixed up with Chet. Told 'em you had him killed. Said you was going after Josh next.'

'What men said this, Rake?'

'Some white mens.'

'What white men? Do you have any names?'

'Never did get straight on that. Just some white mens trying to stir up trouble, I guess.'

'Well, they did that all right.'

'When I tried to stop them boys they knocked me out. Their own coach! But don't you worry none, mister. I'm fixin' to call Mr Jaspers on 'em. He'll set those two right.'

'Mr Jaspers?'

'He owns the Blues. Big colored fella. He'll come down on them two boys real hard. Say, I know you got a right, but I'd be much obliged if you didn't call the police on 'em. They ain't bad boys, just donkey-headed, that's all.'

I held up my hand. 'Don't worry. I don't think the police is just where I want to go right now. You see, I've got a little problem of my own.'

'Thank you, mister, thank you. Here, lemme give you some sides to take with you.' Before I could stop him, he got to his feet and went over to the record bin. 'Seems I remember you saying you was partial to Billy Eckstine. Here we are.' He pulled out two records. 'Billy's latest. And take this here Hamp, too.'

'That's not necessary, Rake.'

'You never mind. These are on the old coach.' He handed the records to me. 'And don't you worry 'bout them two characters of mine. They'll be taken care of all right.'

I offered to give Rake a ride home, but he said he'd rather just sit in the store awhile and listen to some music while his senses came back to him. He told me once more that he would take care of the gunmen who tried to give me a lead transfusion. Fair enough, I thought. It was a whole lot more than the cops would do.

15.

I went to Chinatown for dinner. A joint called Louie's. I parked and walked up Grant Street, Chinatown's main drag. The street was jumping. A few markets were still open and pushing their bok choy, bitter melon and lotus root to last minute shoppers. Copper-colored ducks were turning slowly on spits in delicatessen windows. The smell of soy sauce and fresh fish swirled lazily along the street like a summer fog. Little dark-eyed children in pigtails and cereal bowl haircuts and wispy old people in their traditional dress and slippers jammed the narrow sidewalks. Chinatown. The sound of a language I don't understand, the signs above the shops I can't read and the false pagoda façades to fancy nightclubs I can't afford make me think I'm in a foreign country. I am. But there is also something about Chinatown that makes me feel like I'm in my backyard. Louie's is like that.

I turned off Grant at the Chinese telephone exchange building, leaving the neon lights and jade dragons to the tourists, and walked west on Washington. Louie's is on Old Chinatown Lane just a block up. A narrow little street – an alley really – of shops and bazaars, the Lane used to be known for its gambling parlors and brothels. They say it was a place where you could pull old Buddha's gong for the price of a pack of cigarettes. But that was a long time ago.

Louie's is a little chop suey joint sandwiched between the House of Ming, a jewelry and stone figurine shop, and a Chinese benevolent association. I walked in and took a stool at the counter. I ordered a plate of the usual, exchanged a few words with Frank Louie, the owner and cook, and then buried my nose in plateful of noodles and the evening newspaper.

A small headline at the bottom of the front page caught my eye – 'Police Chief To Quit'. Seems the leader of the city's finest was hanging up his holster after 35 years on the force, the last ten as Chief. It almost read like a eulogy to the man who 'kept our streets safe for more than a decade'. That reporter should've talked to me. I could've pointed out a few streets that weren't all that safe. For me, at least.

I wouldn't have bothered to finish the article, since besides a general lack of interest, it was continued on an inside page. But somewhere between the chop suey and the mushi pork, I found myself on that inside page reading another article. My eyes jumped the column and resumed the waxy eulogy to the soon to be departed chief.

Figuring prominently in the first two paragraphs was the name of Garth Cane. He joined the chorus of those who swore the chief was the best thing to happen to Frisco since the gold rush of '49. But he also said something that sounded curious. When asked who he thought would succeed the chief, he said the new top cop would 'come from inside the department.'

He would not name any names, but he did say the flatfoot with the inside track to the job was 'a family man with a distinguished service record, a veteran officer, a man I would consider it an honor to work with'. Sounded like he was making a nominating speech at a political convention. But the knowledge that a pal of Cane's would be in charge of all those guns and nightsticks made me lose my appetite. And the fortune cookie didn't make me feel any better – 'you will meet new people who will change your life'. I'd like to meet the wiseguy who wrote that and give him a piece of my mind.

I finished off my green tea, paid the freight on the meal

and left. Maybe it was all catching up with me, but Chinatown didn't feel like my backyard anymore. The fact that Garth Cane and the Hall of Justice were only two blocks away made it appear downright unfriendly.

I snaked my way through the crowded streets to my car and took the shortest route home. A big lump set in my throat and it wasn't the chop suey.

Frisco is a small town, but it still took almost 30 minutes to get to my flat. Nothing special waiting for me when I got home. Some long-forgotten bills, a shut-off notice from the phone company, a statement from the Book of the Month Club cancelling my membership for non-payment and a body lying face down on my sofa. I should've expected it – it had been one of those days.

I tossed the mail on the table and went over to get a closer look at the stiff. I rolled it over. It was sergeant Watt with a dark brown hole in his forehead. I stepped back and parked my goods in the easy chair across from the sofa. I shook out a Chesterfield from a nearly empty pack, fired it up and took a pull. What I exhaled was a whole lot more than just cigarette smoke.

I sat in the chair for a long moment staring at the wall. Mother warned me there would be times like this. All those cocky feelings I was beginning to get about solving this case in record quick time now lay dead on my couch.

One thing was clear. This thing did go further up the ladder than Watt. I had the proof right there in front of me in case there were doubters. Somebody had gone to great length to point it out to me. They had also made it clear that the price I was to pay for working on the Chet Jones case was murder or a murder rap or both. Whoever they were, they seemed to be masters of thoroughness.

Speaking of murder rap, I hadn't been home five minutes when I heard the sirens. What timing these guys have.

16.

I was tired of dodging bullets and taking shots to the kidneys from brutes. I don't know, maybe I'm growing old, but I just couldn't run from the cops. Not this time. I was just too beat. So, I sat there smoking a cigarette waiting for them to kick in the door and cuff me off to the klink.

They hustled me down to the Hall of Justice and into one of the interrogation rooms they have to sweat out confessions from desperados. I was left alone for a long time. The room wouldn't win any design prizes from House Beautiful magazine. Bare floor, bare walls, an old wooden table and three or four hard, straight-backed chairs that were built with Presbyterians in mind. Oh, yes, and there was one of those lamps with an inverted funnel hood hanging from a thin cord in the ceiling. It was the type of lamp that cops in the movies use to shine in the eyes of the suspect to break him down.

I sat in one of the chairs. I wanted a smoke something awful, but my hands were still cuffed behind my back. The room was dark except for the 'sweat' lamp which hung like a dead man less than three feet above the table.

About 20 minutes later the door opened. Four men in hats and suits came in. Three of them sat around the table. Two of them were smoking cigarettes, one a cigar, and one was Garth Cane. He sat directly across from me.

'Looks like you didn't take me up on my offer, Kovachs,' he said. His face was partly in the shadows so I couldn't tell whether he was smiling or not.

'How about taking off these bracelets,' I said. 'I won't murder any of you.'

Cane nodded to one of his pals who came over and unlocked the cuffs. I rubbed my wrists to get the circulation going.

'We've got you on murder one, Kovachs,' Cane said. 'There's no way out of this. It'll go easier on you if you tell us about it.'

'Mind if I smoke?'

Cane reached inside his coat for his cigarettes. He slid the pack across the table to me. I ignored them. 'I've got my own,' I said, shaking out a fresh butt. 'Chesterfields. Joe Dimaggio's brand. How about that?'

'You don't seem to realize just how deep a jam you're in, Kovachs,' said the Assistant District Attorney.

I lit my cigarette and threw the match on the floor. 'Why don't you tell me, Cane, and then we'll both know.'

One of Cane's pals, the cop with the cigar, got up from his chair and walked over to me. He grabbed the lamp and turned it into my eyes. 'You killed a cop, Kovachs!' he said. 'You'll fry for it!'

He let go of the lamp. It swung back and forth on its cord, splashing light on angry faces all staring at me. The smoke from their tobacco hung in opaque auras around their faces. They looked like Macbeth's witches in snap brim hats. If I had been the superstitious type I would have jumped through my skin and probably confessed to every unsolved murder on the books. But I stopped believing in ghosts about the same time I tumbled to the Easter Bunny con. Still, three big, ugly cops in gabardine with faces like the inside of a dog food can, standing over the oily pierce-eyed figure of the DA did give a person a chance to change his mind.

'Why'd you do it, Kovachs?' I heard one of the standing voices say.

'We got the gun,' said another.

'You didn't think you could get away with it, did you?' said a third.

Disconnected voices come from the smokey darkness. They were raising the temperature toward the third degree.

'You confess,' said Cane, ' and I can arrange it so they go easy on you. Fifteen years maximum. Maybe half that.'

'He killed a cop,' said one of the disconnected voices. 'I say we push him all the way to the chair.'

'You're going to fry for this, Shamus,' said another voice. The lamp was still swaying, but it never seemed to throw its light on the face that was doing the talking.

'I'm the only friend you've got, Kovachs,' said Cane. This time I could see the smile on his face. A nasty, smug smile. 'The others want to send you to the chair. I don't think a jury would disagree with them. Do you?'

I took a slow drag from my Chesterfield. 'What's the rib, Cane?'

'Rib?'

'Yeah. What's the joke? How about letting me in on the laugh.'

'There ain't nothing funny,' said one of the voices.

'Unless you think a date with old smokey at San Quentin is funny,' said another voice.'

'You don't seriously think I killed Watt?' I said.

'You had a run in with him,' said one of the cops blowing smoke in my face.

'Sure, an that should prove I didn't kill him.'

'Huh?' said the one with the cigar. 'That don't make no sense.'

'Figure it out,' I said. 'If I had a public run-in with Watt, which I did, and I got called on the carpet the next day by Cane, which I did, and had my license pulled, which I did, and was threatened with assault charges, which I was, what do you think happened next? That I called Watt to come over to my place to kiss and make up? But when he showed up I plugged him instead, laid him on my couch and then sat around waiting for the cops to come and pick me up?'

'It could've happened that way,' said one of the voices.

'Give it up, Cane,' I said. 'You can't make it stick and you know it.'

'I can make anything in this town stick.'

'Then maybe you can tell me who murdered Chet Jones.'

'Who's that?'

'Don't play the sap with me, Cane. You and the rest of the boys here know I am working on the Jones case. I used to think Watt killed him, or had him killed. Maybe he did, but that isn't the point.'

'Oh, there is a point to this?'

'Yeah. The point is that you have been going to a lot of trouble to get me to drop this case. I want to know why. Who are you protecting? It isn't Watt anymore. How about Captain Shultz? You protecting him?'

'You're crazy, Kovachs.'

'Tell me something I don't know. Tell me Shultz isn't going to be the new Chief of Police. Tell me he and Watt weren't buddies. Tell me he had nothing to do with Chet Jones's murder.'

'You're hysterical, Kovachs. We're getting nowhere with this. You had your chance.' Cane turned to one of his flunkeys. 'Take him downstairs and lock him up.' Two of them approached me from either side and grabbed my arms.

'Tell me one more thing, Cane,' I said, as I was being escorted to the door.

'You'll be arraigned in the morning,' Cane said, matter-of-factly. 'Murder one.'

'Tell me Shultz wasn't at Port Chicago and Mare Island in '44.'

I could hear a chair scraping across the floor. Then footsteps. It was Cane. He came up and stuck his face into mine. 'I gave you a lot of rope, Kovachs. You had more than one chance. Now it's too late. You're a dead man.' He turned and began walking away. 'Go on,' he said to the two cops on my arms, 'book him.'

'Murder one, right?' said one of the cops.

'No,' said Cane, sarcastically, 'disturbing the peace.' The door opened. 'Wait!' said Cane. 'Book him on assault and release him into his own custody.'

'What?' said the astonished cop. 'You said murder one.'

'I know what I said! Now I'm saying release him. I want this wiseguy out on the streets. I don't want him turning up dead in one of my jail cells. You know how cops get when one of their own is murdered. Yeah, let him walk. If he gets bumped off on the street, then who's to say it's not just another example of the senseless violence that seems to be this city's calling card these days?'

'Are you sure about this?' asked one of the cops.

'You heard me. Book him and then cut him loose. We don't have enough to hold him for more than 72 hours anyway. I wouldn't want to bet he lasts even that long on the streets.'

'Okay,' said one of the cops on my arms.

'Cane,' I said, 'You're swell. I'll return the favor someday.'

'Get him out of here!' the Assistant District Attorney yelled at the top of his voice.

17.

It was past midnight when I got home. The cab driver poured me out of the back of his hack and pointed me towards my front door. I had about as much energy as Hoover Dam during a power workers' strike and the only thing on my mind was mattress and pillow. Not murder, not bigotry, not political cover-up, not potential jail sentences. Just sleep. I got undressed somewhere between the front door and the bedroom. I turned out the light and was stacking lumber before the room had a chance to get dark.

Morning came all too soon. I was hoping when I woke I would realize that yesterday was just a bad dream. But by my second cup of Brazil water I knew better.

My sleepy eyes tried to glim the morning headlines. It was full of the usual stuff – red hordes threatening to overrun Europe, food rationing schemes here at home, a couple of lurid murders. But there was one thing that was fairly new. Hollywood was being tied to a stake by the House Committee on Un-American Activities. Eleven men, mostly screenwriters were being hauled before J. Parnel Thomas and his gang and having their arms twisted as to why they used communist words like 'democracy' and 'share and share alike' in their films and would they kindly fink on everyone they knew to be, or thought to be, or knew or thought used to be a communist or fellow traveler. I mean America has a right to know, correct? Can't be sending its kids to the movies unless it knows they were written by Americans. This red scare stuff, which seemed to start out as just another fad, had turned serious. And this Thomas Committee was promising to turn Hollywood into a cultural Hiroshima. And there was the Tenney Committee doing the same thing to California schools and colleges. Lots of people besides me being put through the wringer. No doubt about that. It was a sign of the times and I didn't like the way it read.

I was just about to turn to the sports pages and see how the Browns stacked up against their opponent for this Sunday's game when I saw a picture on one of the inside pages that caught my eye. It was Garth Cane. The story next to the mug shot announced that the assistant DA had just 'announced his candidacy for mayor on the last day of filing'.

The article went on to say that Cane's candidacy came as 'somewhat of a surprise, but the recent resignation of Police Chief Grogan, one of the Assistant District Attorney's most formidable opponents over the past several years, has cleared the path for Cane to pursue his long-held ambition to be mayor.'

So, there it was. The ladder I was looking for. Cane was more ambitious than a room full of guys all named Machiavelli. Probably explains why he turned me loose the night before. Didn't want to have to answer any embarrassing questions if I had happened to get lucky and make bail. But it didn't explain why he wanted me to drop the Chet Jones case. What did the death of a Negro warehouseman baseball player have to do with the political career of a man who had stabbed more backs than a Chinatown acupuncturist? Was Watt one of those backs? More importantly, was I going to be?

I had a third cup of murk and a piece of very well-done toast that looked more like a hunk of the stuff they pay people in West Virginia to dig out of the ground. I washed everything down with a glass of old bossy and was out of the house.

The game was more than eight hours away and it was

seven hours until I was supposed to meet Vernell Leggett in Satchel Paige's dressing room. Plenty of time for things like doing the laundry or taking in the double matinée at the Embassy, but not much time to stop race riots and crack open hushed-up cases of corruption.

I had put out the word to Leggett and Nate Murphy and their crowd concerning the former. It was about all I could do. For the latter, I felt like I was on an escalator to nowhere. I knew Cane was protecting someone. I had thought it was Watt and maybe Shultz. Now I wasn't sure. I couldn't picture him mixed up with slack-jaws like Duffy and Myron who between them had the intelligence of a five-pound bag of lawn fertilizer. Cane just didn't seem to be the type. Besides he was much too careful for that sort of thing.

All the ifs, buts and maybes were putting my brain through the spin cycle and it hurt. The only person I could think of going to that might help was the man who seemed to have nothing to do with any of this.

Chief Grogan lived in Pacific Heights among many of his senior crime-fighting, civil serving and politician make-out artist colleagues. Maybe it was going too far to say Pacific Heights was a ghetto for the city's power structure, but you were getting close.

I phoned the chief and told him I was a journalist doing a retrospective profile on him for one of the national crime magazines. When I asked him if he would be available for an interview, I might as well have drawn the winning number during bingo night at St Kevin's. Here was a cop with an ego as large as the Blarney Stone.

It was early afternoon when I got to Grogan's place. He greeted me himself at the door. Tall, leathery, about 60 years old with a back as straight as a pool cue, Frisco's soon-to-be-retired top cop shook my hand and invited me inside.

He led me into his study which was full of stuffed chairs

and animal heads as well as a dozens of mementos from his decades on the force. Mounted photographs of him and politicians, him and celebrities, and him and underprivileged kids competed for wall space with plaques proclaiming meritorious service and pennants from various law enforcement campaigns.

Chief Grogan was a gracious host. He poured me a tumbler of Irish whisky strong enough to win its own bar fights. I told him my name was Riley – Seamus Riley – and that, along with the whisky, helped loosen the chief's tongue. I listened to him ramble on about his career from rookie cop on the beat in the Tenderloin to chief of the force and political poohbah to be reckoned with.

He stopped for a moment to refill his glass. It was the third time. I took the lull to refocus him and get down to cases. 'Your resignation took a lot of people by surprise,' I said, trying to sound like a journalist. 'Was it something you had been planning to do, or was it as sudden as it seemed?'

Grogan inhaled a quarter of the juice in his glass. 'Ah,' he said. 'A truly superior beverage. It's imported, you know. I won't allow any of that domestic rot in the house. Pour it right down the sink if I ever see it.' The chief was beginning to repeat himself. That was the third time he told me his booze was imported from the old country. I was beginning to feel like I was attending a trade show of Irish distillers.

'About your resignation, chief,' I said again, trying to bring him back to this country.

'Hell no, I wasn't planning to resign! I had two more years to go before my retirement.'

'What changed your mind?'

'Changed my mind? Ha! That's a good one. I'll tell you Seamus, my boy, they kicked me out. Me, Dennis Grogan!'

'Who kicked you out?'

Grogan took another gulp from his glass. 'It'll all come out sooner or later anyway. I'm not talking out of school. No atomic secrets to hide.' He giggled at his small joke.

'Chief.'

'It's politics. Everything in this town is politics. You know, the power boys. They decided to back another horse. Guess I should've seen it coming. It's been brewing for a while.'

'Something inside the department?'

'Inside and out. Some of the young Turks have been after my head ever since they got back from the war. Big war heroes. Thought the world owed them a living. Hell, I was a war hero, too. Only for me it was the wrong war. They forget what people like me did for the country in World War I.'

'Anyone in particular have a grudge against you, chief?'

'Hell, you name them. Bosley, Markham, Shultz, O'Brien. O'Brien, that one hurts the most. I knew his father in the old country. We both come from the same county.'

'Shultz. Isn't he going to be the new chief?'

'Yeah. Say, how'd you know that? I thought that was still top secret.'

'I have my sources.' I gave the chief a wink. It seemed to suffice.

'Yeah, Shultz and his war buddies. What a sorry bunch. War heroes. Christ, most of them were godamn military cops guarding American bases. Never killed any Krauts or Japs. What do you think about that?'

'The scum.'

'You're damn tootin' they are.'

'Who's backing them up outside the department, chief?'

Grogan drained what remained in his glass. He would have got up to pour himself another round but he was a little too tight for that. He decided to just sit in his chair and supply me with answers. 'The same goddamn politicos that used to back me. Southern Pacific, the Chamber of Commerce, the Nob Hill crowd, the shipping industry. You name them. I had them all in my corner. Except Cane and his crowd. Slimy sonofabitch has been plotting against me ever since he came into the DA's office.'

'How'd they get away with it? I mean a man with your record and connections. There must have been something to get them to turn on you.'

'Hell, like I said, this has been a long time coming. All they needed was a lousy excuse. Anything to give me the bum's rush.'

'I assume they found one.'

'About a week ago, no, more like two, some of these young Turk cops went crazy on the picket line at Sears. The strike, you know. Beat up some of the pickets pretty bad. One of them in particular went way over his head. Beat some of them senseless. One of them was a nigger. Couple of days later this same colored boy turns up dead at Pacific Shipyard. It came through channels that this same crazy cop who beat him and the others might have had something to do with this colored boy's death.

'I'm no goddamn nigger-lover, but I ordered a departmental investigation. You know, public relations. There could've been a stink if I had ignored it. Besides, I don't want any crazy cops working for me. Well, the next thing I know, everybody is accusing me of hurting department morale. Shit, it was just a lousy goddamn excuse to stick it to the old chief. My supporters melted away overnight and I didn't have a friend to go to bat for me. Cane had pulled the rug out from under me. Now the bastard has announced he is running for mayor. He had it planned all along, the sonofabitch. It's a nasty world out there, Seamus. If you drop your guard for one second, there is some bastard standing by just waiting to throw you to the wolves. You know what I mean?'

I did, and how. The chief began talking about truth, justice and the American way. His speech was turning to slush. He was blotto. Time for me to leave. I got up, shook his hand, thanked him for the interview and left him sitting in his chair looking like a bowl of yesterday's vegetables. It was 4 p.m. I walked out on to the street hoping I could avoid the wolves at least until game time.

18.

I got to Seals Stadium at 6 p.m. on the dot. Night had fallen and the stadium lights were burning brightly. But other than a few ballpark cops, the grounds crew and some of the players who were beginning to arrive, the place was as empty as a Hollywood agent's promise.

I asked one of the cops where the Paige all-stars locker room was located. He pointed me to a runway under the stands. I had no trouble finding it. The door to the room was locked. I gave it a rap and it opened almost immediately. I would have stepped in, but replacing the door was something just as wide and formidable. A mountain of a man, dark and unamused, blocked the entire frame. He looked like the kind of brawn that dined on engine blocks and cleaned his teeth with steel wool.

'What d'ya want?' he said, like if I didn't come up with the right answer it might be my last.

'I'm here for the interview,' I said. 'I'm a friend of Vernell Leggett. He's expecting me. Name's Kovachs.' I hoped that was the right answer.

The large Negro turned his head away from me. 'Hey Leggett,' he called into the room. 'You know a white man calls hisself Kovachs?'

From inside the room I heard a familiar voice. 'Riley, my man. Is that you? Let him in Louis.'

Louis stepped aside and I entered the locker room. Fifteen men, both Negro and white, some with cameras around their necks, were milling about, sitting on benches smoking cigarettes and talking with each other. Vernell informed me that the legendary hurler hadn't arrived yet. I lit a Chesterfield, but before I threw the match away, Leroy 'Satchel' Paige came through the door. Immediately, flash bulbs started popping. The reporters crowded around him.

'Take it easy, boys,' said the tall, lanky object of their attention. 'Jes' lemme set down here and take a load offa my feet.' He eased himself slowly on to the wood bench like a man twice the age of his rumored forty plus years.

'Satch, do you think you can pitch a full nine innings tonight?' piped a voice from the tight little knot of reporters surrounding Satchel Paige.

'Well,' drawled the pitcher. 'as y'all know, ol' Satch most usually only goes three or five innings. But Bobby Feller done issued me a challenge to go the distance with him, so I reckon I'll bc out on the mound when the ninth rolls around.'

'Do you think you can beat Feller?' asked another.

'Well, I done it before, so I reckon I can do it again. Won't know, though 'till the game's over.'

'Satch,' said a third reporter, a black man. 'Now that Jackie Robinson is in the major leagues, do you think you'll get the call to move up?'

Satchel Paige reached in his coat pocket for a cigarette. One of the reporters gave him a light from a silver-colored Zippo.

'Well, that all depends,' he said, through a small, swirling cloud of smoke. 'I been ready for 20 years. They's some who says ol' Satch is too old to pitch major league ball. I guess I'm old, all right, but there's still plenty 'a zip left in the ol' soupbone. You can believe that. Sure, I can pitch in the majors. Been squarin' off against their all-stars every year on the barnstormin' tour. Whuppin' 'em, too. But they'll have to come to me real pretty-like if they want me. They've been puttin' ol' Satch off too long to jes' wiggle their fingers at me now. But I'm ready to go. Have been since '26 or thereabouts.'

'Satch!' another reporter called out. It was Vernell

Leggett. 'The color bar has kept the black man out of major league baseball until now. If full integration is still several years off, aren't the older Negro ball players like yourself likely to grow more and more bitter playing against, and beating, the best the major leagues have to offer while age and discrimination denies them their chance to play in the majors?'

Satchel Paige shook his head and smiled. 'Now that was a mouthful of words, young man. Took all ol' Satch's strength jes' to keep up with you.' The reporters giggled. 'But if I understands your meanin', you want to know if ol' timers like me is angry whuppin' them big leaguers an' not bein' allowed to play with 'em in the regular season. Well, the answer to that one is – yes. I get mad when I stop and think about it. But I'm a pitcher an' that takes all my concentration. It ain't good for the health to be riled up an' all the time mad at a situation you didn't make an' sure as heck can't change all by yourself. Someday, things'll be different an' we'll all get our chance. But until Jim Crow is kicked clean outa baseball, the barnstorm tour is the onliest game in town.'

The interview went on for ten or fifteen more minutes. The reporters wanted to know how the legendary mound ace prepared for big games, what he ate for dinner and if his arm got sore from pitching so often. Satchel Paige playfully answered these and other questions. He was a man who knew how to keep pinpoint control of more than just a fastball and he was every inch a showman as he was a pitcher.

The reporters were shooed away at 7 p.m. when the promoter for the Paige all-stars stepped in and hustled Satch to his locker so he could dress for the game. I left the locker room with Vernell Leggett and accompanied him up to the stadium press box.

It was less than half an hour to game time. The stands, which seat 20,000 were nearly half full. Half way up to the press box I stopped to take a look at the filling house. Loud banging noises coming from behind the third base dugout drew my attention. Several early game revelers were standing up waving open bottles of beer. Others were pounding shiny new garbage can lids with metal spoons. It was the boys from the Purity League. Their contingent appeared to number about 50.

I poked Vernell Leggett in the side. 'Down there,' I pointed. 'Those red-eyed yahoos making all the noise. Those are the clowns I was telling you about. Keep your eye on them. They could spell trouble.'

Leggett nodded while scowling contemptuously in their direction. He turned and continued up the steps to the press box. I followed.

'I know a guy from the *Pittsburgh Courier*,' he told me, as we approached our destination. 'He is an expert on Paige and the Negro leagues. He's been travelling with Satch on the barnstorming tour for years. He'll have some good stuff I can use in the story. We'll sit with him for a couple of innings. I'm sure he'd like to hear about your bigots down there. I told some folks what you told me. They might come by later.'

We reached the press box. Down at the far end were a couple of spaces reserved for 'colored press'. A sign said so. Leggett spotted his friend among three Negro journalists seated at the corner of the press table. 'Preston, my man!' he said.

The man looked up from the newspaper he was reading. 'Vernell Leggett,' he said. He stood up and stuck out his hand. 'Good to see you, man. Since when are you doing sports?'

Leggett took the other man's hand and shook it. 'Since tonight. Our sports editor is home with a bad case of female trouble. The *Sun* sent me over to cover the game. I was hoping you could give me some inside dope on Satchel. You know to fill out the story.'

Leggett pulled up a chair and started to ask questions about Satchel Paige. I just stood behind him like a big dummy. Preston noticed that I wasn't going away. 'Your friend with the *Sun*?' he asked quizzically after a minute.

'Friend?' said Leggett, like the word had just been freshly coined and he was groping around for a meaning. Preston pointed to me with his eyes. Leggett turned around in his chair. 'Oh, Jesus! Kovachs! I'm sorry. Preston Cobb, journalist, meet Riley Kovachs, private eye.'

'Private eye?' said Cobb. 'Leggett, you got a bodyguard these days? I knew that big mouth of yours was going to get you in trouble sooner or later, but a bodyguard!'

'Ain't nothin' like that, Preston. Kovachs is working on the case of a brother who was killed last week. A star player for the Blues. And what do you mean "big mouth"?'

Preston Cobb ignored Leggett and spoke directly to me. 'You mean Chet Jones?'

I nodded.

'I heard the kid died in an accident. Fell off a ship or something.'

'Shows what you know, Mr Drew Pearson with a black face,' Leggett said. 'Go ahead, Kovachs. Tell him about that group of hyenas down there.'

For the next five minutes I told him the clipped version of the Pacific Coast Purity League, its link with Chet Jones's death and their plans, such as I knew them, for the upcoming game. I told him that people should keep an eye on Josh Williams and suggested the reporter might want to get word to him and the rest of the Negro all-stars before the game started. I didn't want to start panic, because for all I knew, Duffy and his beer buddies would just raise a bit of a stink then go home drunk, rather than start a race riot.

Preston Cobb absorbed everything I told him and added some of his own. He related the news about the Pacific Coast Purity League to the threats against Jackie

Robinson that had followed him all through the season. He said they were just hollow bellowings from a handful of bigots, but all had to be taken seriously. Not wise to take any chances, he said. He picked up his newspaper from the press table and got up to leave.

'There's some people down on the field who should know about this,' he said.

'May I make a suggestion?' I asked. 'There's this large . . .'

'You mean Louis? He's the first person, I'm going to talk to.'

The three of us walked out of the press box and down the stadium steps toward the Paige all-stars dugout. Along the way, Preston Cobb supplied Vernell Leggett with some of the facts that accompany the legend about Satchel Paige. He told him he'd been travelling with the all-stars since the barnstorming tour began more than a month ago. He saw 'the old man' as he called Paige, outpitch Ewell Blackwell. Twice! That was the same Ewell Blackwell who won 22 games this season for a mediocre Cincinnati team. One of those victories was a no-hitter against Boston. More recently, he said, Paige had gone head to head with 'Rapid Robert' Feller. The American league's only 20-game winner in 1947, he reminded us. This was the same Bob Feller who set a major league record last year when he struck out 348 batters. That, I already knew.

The veteran reporter told us that although the Paige all-stars lost the two games with Feller's boys, Satch outpitched the American league's premier pitcher. 'Feller gave up seven hits and struck out the same number in nine innings of pitching. Satchel, over those same nine innings, gave up five hits and one run while fanning fifteen! Fifteen strike outs!' Cobb exclaimed. 'Against big leaguers like Kiner, Pafko, Fain and Keltner. The man is in his prime, I tell you. It'll be a goddamn crime if he doesn't get a chance to play in the majors.'

Preston Cobb left us when we reached field level. He

gave Vernell Leggett his press packet and line-up card. Then he stepped over the railing and disappeared into the Paige all-stars dugout. Leggett and I walked back up the steps several rows to his seats which were between home plate and the retinue of race-haters. It was a few minutes past 7.30 p.m.

Five minutes later the Negro team took the field. A crescendo of boos and loud clanging noises rose from the Purity League contingent. It was heard by everyone in the stadium. But there was also a hearty moment of applause from the predominantly white grandstands. When Satchel Paige reached the mound a few moments later and picked up the ball, the crowd drowned out the booing and hooting in a loud demonstration of approval. A half a dozen warm-up pitches later, the game was under way.

Peanuts Lowry was the lead-off batter for the Feller all-stars. Paige made him look bad as he threw a steady dose of fast balls past him. Peanuts, the Chicago Cubs right fielder, went down swinging, connecting with nothing but the night air. The next two batters followed suit. Satchel made it all look so easy. The crowd roared as he strolled to the dugout.

Feller wasn't so lucky in his half of the first. The Paige's got to 'Rapid Robert's' blazing blue fast ball for three consecutive hits and a run.

In the second, Satchel Paige, employing his famed assortment of pitches – from the 'hesitation' and the 'bee ball' to 'Long Tom' and the 'trouble ball' – put away the major league batsmen in order without working up a sweat. Josh Williams led of the bottom of the inning. Most of the fans gave him a robust 'home-town boy' round of applause. The Purity Leaguers, on the other hand, let loose a barrage of insults that carried well beyond their little 'rooting' section.

'Hey snowflake!' some base-voiced bigot bellowed. 'I saw your momma in a tree last night.'

'Hey shine!' yelled another. 'We can smell you from up here.' The Jim Crowers laughed and beat on their can lids. Some people not with Duffy's crowd told them to shut up.

Josh picked on a Feller fast ball and drove it deep to left field. But it wasn't hit far enough to do any damage and the left fielder hauled it in after a brief chase. Duffy and Myron's contingent roared with satisfaction as the ball was thrown back to the infield, and let fly with another round of racial taunts.

But their joy was short lived. Joe Greene, the catcher was the next batter. He took a Feller fast ball 'downtown' as they say. A booming homerun that put the Paige's up 2-0.

In the third, the Purity Leaguers started hooting at Paige. 'Hey, Uncle Remus,' cried one of the loudmouths. 'You should be home pickin' cotton.'

'Hey Satch!' another yelled through cupped hands. 'Why don't you throw your watermelon ball?'

A couple of fans a few rows back of the Purity League crowd shouted back, 'Shut up and watch the game.' A moment later a small shoving match between three or four white fans flared briefly.

I don't know if any of the taunts got to Satchel Paige. He had heard it all before – a thousand times – but Bob Sturgeon of the Cubs led off with a line drive double off the fence. Then the Negro mound ace reached into his bag of tricks and came up with a combination of speed and mixed wind-ups to strike out the next three batters.

In the home half of the third, Feller's infield unravelled. Two errors and four hits, including a single by Josh Williams, produced four runs for the Paige all-stars.

A hush fell over Duffy's pepsters. They themselves became the recipients of taunts from some of the fans. After the Paige's had pushed across their seventh run of the game, one man, a white man, stood up and bellowed 'Hey, you Jim Crowers! Eat Crow!' Several dozen around him took it up and chanted it a number of times to emphasize their point. The only noise coming from the once-boisterous segregationists was an occasional 'Shudd-up!' in response to catcalls from the fans.

These fans were probably distant from, if not hostile to, the views of militant integrationists, and not likely progressive-minded in the literal sense of the word. They were just everyday folk with an old-fashioned sense of justice. People who enjoy baseball and appreciate talent. It didn't much matter to them if the outstanding performers were white or black. The game's the thing to them. Too bad they couldn't get that message through to the eucalyptus-headed moguls of the game waiting for Branch Rickey's Robinson 'experiment' to fall flat on its face.

The Paige all-stars scored another run in the bottom of the eighth. Satch was pitching like a man half his age. He was throwing 'aspirin tablets', as the sports scribes like to say when referring to fast ball pitchers who are hot. Ol' man Paige was certainly that. He retired the side in order in the ninth. For the game, he had given up four hits, no runs and struck out fifteen. In fairness to Feller, the team he fielded was a cut below some of the squads he had put together in the past. But they were major league ball players and Satchel Paige and his stars had thumped them 8-0!

The old man of the hill had outpitched the best pitcher in the big leagues for the third time in less than a month. And Josh Williams. He stroked a second single in the eighth inning and made a near-impossible catch of a line drive to the left field corner that brought the crowd to its feet. If Mr Bill Veeck, the new owner of the Cleveland Indians, was in the stands as was rumored, I hope he took a good hard look at two generations of talent out there on the playing field. I think just about everyone at Seals Stadium, the Purity League crowd included, would have to agree that it wasn't lack of ability that was keeping Satchel Paige and Josh Williams out of major league baseball.

19.

The fans filed out of the stands quickly. In 15 minutes nearly everyone had emptied into the side streets of Potrero Hill and were on their way home. Only a few hundred stragglers remained. They included a dozen young boys who ran from aisle to aisle looking for empty paper cups to turn upside down and stomp on. The hollow booming of the cups reverberated throughout the wood and cement arena.

Twenty minutes after that, all cups popped, bets paid off and after-game places to go decided upon, the stadium stood virtually deserted. Vernell Leggett and I walked out of the ball park and down the Bryant Street side of the stadium toward 15th. We stood in front of a side door from which players were straggling out a few at a time.

The stadium lamps high above the outfield threw enough light so that we could see across the street, but not much farther. Both Leggett and I lit cigarettes. It seemed like the right thing to do. Then, suddenly, the stadium ground crew, their work done for the evening, doused the lights. The whole block was plunged into darkness. A cloudy moon, the dim, yellow glow from downtown lights, a naked bulb over the players exit and the reddened tips of our tobacco gave the only light for 100 feet in any direction.

Vernell Leggett and I said nothing to each other about anything. But we were both thinking the same thing. After a few minutes standing in the dark the players' door opened. Two men walked out. I could barely make out their faces, but I knew that one of them was Levi Williams. The man at his side was his son, Josh. Without a word to each other, Leggett and I started toward them.

'Mr Williams,' I said as we got to mutual recognition range. 'Mind if Mr Leggett, here, and I walk with you to your car?'

'Kovachs!' said the older Williams, angrily. 'I told you I didn't want you messin' in my business. Now leave me an' my boy be.'

He started to push past us. Vernell Leggett offered his opinion. 'Hold on there, Williams,' he said. 'There's been some threats made against your son. Kovachs is just trying to help you look out for him. You could give in a little on that, couldn't you? I mean, no need to take the man's head off.'

Levi Williams stopped and turned sharply in Leggett's direction. 'I don't know you at all,' he said, sticking an angry finger in his face. 'But I'll tell you what I told that big fool Louis, inside. Leave us alone! We can take care of ourselves!'

Vernell Leggett threw up his hands and shrugged his shoulders. 'Well, mister, you just may be right. I hope for your sake and that boy's there, you are.' He turned to me. 'Come on Kovachs, let's blow. No good samaratins needed around here.'

The four of us parted. Vernell and I had gone only about 20 yeard when we heard voices. Loud voices. We turned to see a flashlight bobbing up and down at the head of an undetermined number of people. They were coming from the direction of the Short Stop Bar, and were coming fast. In a second they had formed a half-circle around Josh and Levi Williams. The man carrying the flashlight was Duffy. His pals numbered at least 20. They were drunk and angry.

They moved back and forth in front of the Williams men blocking their way. Insults flowed from their lips like raw sewage into the Bay. Some banged the ground with wooden clubs and tyre irons.

'Looks like we caught us a couple niggers.' I heard Duffy say as he shone the light in Josh and Levi Williams's faces.

Leggett and I came running up behind the two quarried men. 'Call it off, Duffy!' I said.

The blond-haired bigot recognized me. 'Well, well,' he said smiling, 'this must be our lucky day. Look who's here, boys. It's that nigger-lovin' spy who crashed our meetin'.' Duffy's confederates growled like bad-tempered dogs on short leashes.

'An' he brought his own coon with 'im,' laughed another, pointing at Leggett.

Then another man stepped up alongside Duffy. 'Looks like we're goin' to have a real nice little party,' he said, tapping a baseball bat across his open palm. 'Goin' to teach 'em a good lesson about the nigger's place in major league baseball. I get first dibs on the white creep,' he said, almost snorting the words.

The four of us – Vernell Leggett, the two Williams men and me – looked at each other and knew without saying anything, there was only one way out of this. We spread out slightly, squared off and mentally picked out spots in the line of men in front that we wanted to hit.

Duffy's maulers were a bit tentative. They continued to call us names and threatened that horrible tortures were in store of us and our women and anybody who ever had anything to do with us. We waited for them to make a move. It seemed like we were waiting an eternity, but in truth, the whole scene up to that point had taken less than three minutes.

I got tired of waiting. Get it over with, that's my motto when it comes to pain. 'Geronimo!' I yelled and took a running dive at the enemy line. It took them all by surprise. I plowed into one beefy character, bowling him over and taking two or three others with him. Then my luck began to take a big turn for the worse. A couple of the Purity League bruisers jumped on my back and began pounding my head and kidneys.

I heard Levi Williams call out, 'I'll take that skinny one with the yellow hair,' referring to Duffy, 'and the one next to him. Son, you know what to do.'

In the next second a free-for-all was in full swing. I had regained my feet momentarily. I took aim on my guy who was just then getting up and clouted him square on his big, ugly kisser. Then, from the corner of my eye, I saw another thug with a tyre iron raised directly above my head. I knew there wasn't time to avoid its murderous plunge. I turned and looked up at it dumbly while trying to raise my arms to protect my head. The iron had reached its upward arc and was slowly beginning its descent to my head. Then a big black hand came from nowhere and grabbed the arm wielding the iron, stopping it cold. The hand belonged to Levi Williams. He yanked the man with the tyre iron and unloaded a 100-pound fist on his jaw. The man crumbled like a soda cracker in a bowl of hot soup.

A shrill scream came from behind me. 'Get the niggers!' I turned to look. It was Myron, the hardware store owner. Then, I took a baseball bat in my stomach. I doubled over and gasped for air. Vernell Leggett fell at me feet, blood streaming down the side of his face. I tried to help him up, but I was hit once again and fell on top of him instead.

I rolled off and saw two goons holding Josh Williams while a third was punching him in the face and stomach. Levi Williams was next to them with two men on his back and one around each leg. But he still found the strength to plant his very large fists into those hostile white faces within his range.

'Kill the niggers! Kill the niggers!' The bloodthirsty chant rang in my ears as I struggled to my feet and stumbled in the direction where Josh Williams was being worked over. I pulled one man off him, but was hopelessly outmatched. It looked like Josh was just going to have to take a beating. We all were.

Then I heard some more shouting. A different, louder chanting. 'Get the racists! Get the fascists!' Duffy's gang stopped dead in their collective tracks and turned in the direction of the chanting. I peered out into the darkness and saw 40 men coming at us. They were marching as if in formation. Then they broke ranks and surrounded our little bloody melée.

'Preston!' exclaimed Vernell Leggett, getting to his feet with some difficulty. 'Coffee Ship Charlie! That you, brother?' I could see the cavalry had come to the rescue. More than half the fresh troops were Negroes. And it looked like at least that many were wearing longshoremen's caps. 'We could use a little assistance to help clean up this pack of garbage pails,' Leggett said.

Without another word, the men waded into Duffy's gang, throwing fist after loaded fist. Louis, the giant security guard for the Paige all-stars, picked up one of the Purity League stout-hearts and threw him into a crowd of four or five of his brothers. They all went down and Louis made sure they stayed down by throwing his drop hammer fists into the flesh of any who foolishly dared rise to his feet.

Out of the corner of my eye I saw Nate Murphy and shouted to him. The blood was flowing like wine at a French wedding. Only this time it wasn't ours. Duffy's scurvy dozens were hollering bloody murder and trying desperately to escape. But our boys had them surround ed and weren't about to let them off so easily. Two bigots in matching high school letter jackets went down under a rain of blows from father and son Williams, who looked like a drum combo playing their own arrangement of 'Cherokee'.

The next five minutes were almost fun. The sound of knuckles cracking bone and labanzas being emptied of air, and in some cases, beer, was all in our favor. The racists were outnumbered and outmuscled. There was a certain satisfaction giving Duffy and his crowd the old one-two without suffering so much as a Bronx cheer in return. I'm sure some of the others felt the same way. Josh Williams had a bloodied high school letterman by the collar of his red and white jacket. He reached back and let him have the sandman special right on his jaw. 'That's for keepin' Buck Leonard out of the majors,' he said, just as he connected. The man wheeled around like a shopping cart out of control. Josh grabbed him by the collar once more. 'And this is for keepin' Satchel out,' he said, delivering the punch that put out his lights.

Almost spontaneously, the fighting ceased. Vernell Leggett walked up to a bloody, puffy-eyed Duffy. He put his hands on his hips as he walked around the battered bigot. 'Well, well, well,' Leggett mocked. 'What have we got here? A puny peckerwood with his stuffings kicked out.' He jabbed a finger into Duffy's chest almost knocking him over. 'Now, you listen real good. I want you to pick up all this white trash sewage around here and cart it away before we turn the lot of you into dog food. Understand me, boy?' Duffy nodded. 'What?' yelled Leggett right into his face.

'Yes,' said the semi-conscious Duffy.

'Yes, what?'

'Yes, sir.'

Vernell Leggett grinned and turned to me. 'I just love it when they call you sir.' He returned to Duffy. 'Now, you get your mangey butt outa here. Scat!' Duffy began stumbling away in the direction of the Short Stop Bar. 'And don't let us catch you or any of your segregationist popcorn-heads around this ball park ever again.' Leggett then turned to me and whispered, 'Hold me up, Kovachs,

I think I'm going to faint.' I did and he didn't, but we were both pretty busted up. A couple of Leggett's longshore pals took him under the arms and walked him to a waiting car at the curb.

'We were great, weren't we, Kovachs?' he said as he was being helped into the car.

'The best,' I said trying to crack a smile. But it hurt too much. Everything I had hurt. Even my eyelashes. And if the truth were known, I never wanted to 'team up' with Vernell Leggett or anyone else for that matter, ever again. Even if we were guaranteed to win. I waved to Vernell with my eyes as the car drove off.

Nate Murphy came over and offered to drive me home. I told him I could make it on my own if rigor mortis didn't set in. I thanked him for showing up and pitching in.

'Just between you and me, Riley,' he said out of the corner of his mouth in a lowered voice, 'I'm here on my own. I brought a couple of the boys from Sears, but this wasn't sanctioned by the Party. The Political Committee said it was "politically incorrect to intervene in this manner". To hell with 'em. I'll get in a lot of hot water for coming here, but what the hell, it was worth it, pal.'

'I'm beginning to like you, Murphy,' I said, giving him a comradely pat on his shoulder. 'I think there's hope for you yet.'

'And you too, pal,' he said with a smile.

'Touché, old man. Touché. Now, if you will excuse me, I have a heavy date with a cup of coffee and a very hot bath.'

I shook Nate Murphy's hand and started off slowly toward my car, like an old man walking on a bed of soft boiled eggs. I only got about 15 yards when I heard someone call my name. It was Levi Williams.

'You handled yourself pretty good out there,' he said. 'First time in my life I ever saw white men fightin' over black men.' His face was sober and stoney. There was a trace of bewilderment in his voice.

'We're not all bigots,' I said. 'It just seems that way most of the time.'

Levi Williams shook his head. 'White men fightin' *with* colored men an' not against them.'

'It happens, Mr Williams. Not often, but it does happen.'

'Yeah, I guess so. What I'm tryin' to say is maybe I was wrong about you.'

I held up my hands. 'No need to apologize.'

'I ain't apologizin'!' he said sharply. 'I said maybe I was wrong. I got 46 years that say different from what I seen tonight. But one thing I got to say.' He hesitated and looked away from me. The basso profundo call of a ship in the Bay filled the awkward silence. 'Your buttin' in on Josh an' me tonight after I told you I don't know how many times to stay clear of us. Well, I'm glad you done what you done.'

Levi Williams turned as soon as the last word was out of his mouth and walked away. Down toward 15th Street where he joined Josh. I watched both men until they disappeared into the foggy dark. But I could still hear their footsteps. They grew fainter and finally, they too, were gone. I reached into my pocket for a Chesterfield. I lit it and took a pull. A long pull. Somewhere a cat was rattling through some garbage cans. No other sound. No cars, no buses, no mothers yelling at their kids to turn out the lights and go to bed. No nothing.

20.

I slept to almost ten the next morning. I lay in bed for the next hour counting my aches and going over what I would do to put the wraps on the Chet Jones case. First, I would go over to the ILWU hall and turn over the information I had about a couple of Duffy's Purity Leaguers who work at Pacific Shipyard. I would also tell them about a cop named Watt. I would tell them that he's dead, but the bosses aren't. I would tell them that police captain Shultz and assistant district attorney Cane are behind it all.

Shultz most definitely was tied into the Purity League through Watt and I would bet dollars to donuts that he gave the word to Watt and his pals to set up the murder of Chet Jones. Settling an old war time grudge was the motive. That and a bigot's commitment to protect 'the white man's game'.

Cane's role was to lay a rug over the whole thing and he would have succeeded if I had not talked to Luke Cornell and linked both Watt and Shultz to Chet Jones through the mutiny at Mare Island. Cane's motives were different than Shultz's but just as personal. He had to protect Shultz who was a key figure in his road to the mayor's office. Shultz had engineered the ouster of chief Grogan which paved the way for the assistant DA. Covering up a little thing like murder was no great price to pay to save a well-planned political career. In fact it was two murders. When it looked like I was on to Watt, Cane had him bumped off to prevent him from spilling the beans and implicating Shultz, Cane's choice for Grogan's replacement.

Murder and bribery. It was obvious that Cane got to his friends at Pacific Shipyards to cough up some hush money to keep Ruby Jones quiet.

With all this in their laps, the ILWU would have plenty to at least open a cause-of-death investigation at Pacific. What they could do about Shultz and Cane only time would tell. Hopefully, not too much time. Decent folks have been waiting long enough to settle accounts with the Shultzes and Canes of the world.

After talking with the longshoremen I would go back to see Ruby Jones and try to explain it all to her. I would tell her why her husband died. I would also tell her that barring a monumental cover-up by the police and District Attorney's office – and I would tell her that was a real possibility – she could look forward to the company being made to pay out a lot more money in survivors' benefits.

Not very neat – the wrapping up of this case – but that's the way most of them are. If the union is a bulldog about seeing justice done and Ruby Jones and her kids being taken care of, it might have a good ending.

Racial justice was something else. Just how long must America be run by Jim Crow and his pals from the Short Stop Bar to the White House? I couldn't answer that one. It's one story that won't have a good ending. Not today. Not in October 1947. But then Jackie Robinson broke the color bar this year and set professional baseball on fire. Torched a lot of traditions and old time notions about a lot of things. He was in the majors to stay and more Negro ball players would follow him. And that counted for something. Maybe it counted for a lot.

I got the pains under control one more time and rolled out of bed, dressed and dragged the razor across my stubble. I had things to do. I was sitting in the kitchen sipping my first cup of grounds. The sun sprayed lemony rays of warmth through the window and on to my face. It felt good. I walked to the window and threw it open and took a great big drink of the outdoors. The sky was blue, the clouds white and the sun high. It was one of those picture postcard days that folks on the street stop one another to talk about. It was the kind of day even independent-minded, hard-boiled detectives could not pass up.

I tossed a hunk of Swiss cheese and an apple into a paper bag and walked out the door. There was this bluff overlooking the ocean at Fort Funston that demanded my immediate presence. There, among the thick and luxurious beach grass, I would sit and regard the firmament. Justice would be glad to wait another hour.

•